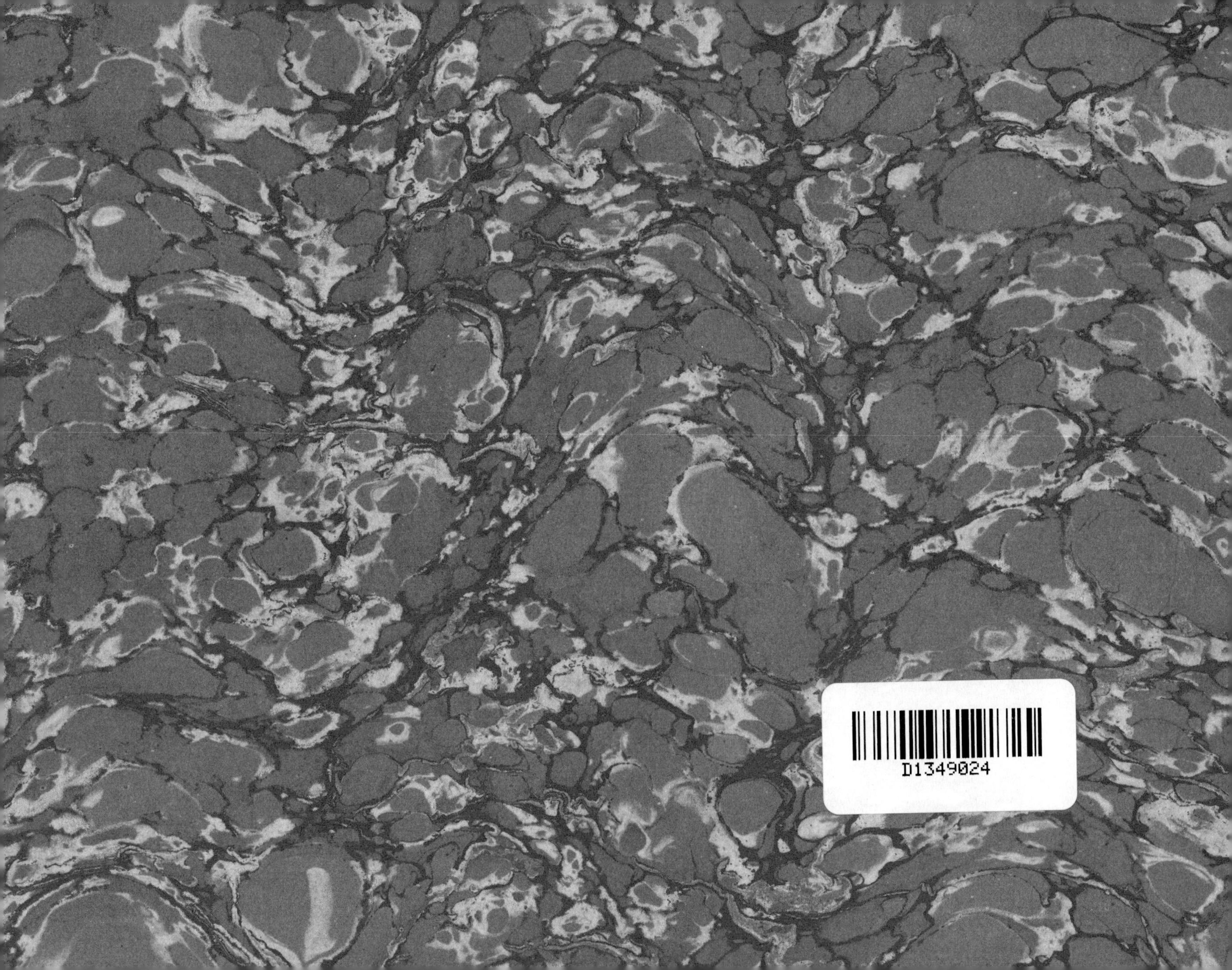

RIDING HIGH

RIDING HIGH

1896-1903

Scenes from a Lakeland Childhood

Barbara Sneyd

Adapted by Phyllida Barstow

Pelham Books
London

First published in Great Britain in 1986 by Pelham Books Limited
27 Wrights Lane, Kensington, London W8 5DZ

Published simultaneously in the United States by Dodd, Mead & Company, Inc. New York

Riding High was conceived, edited and designed by Thames Head Limited
Avening, Tetbury, Gloucestershire, Great Britain

Editorial and Marketing Director
Martin Marix Evans

Design and Production Director
David Playne

Art Editor
Barry Chadwick

Editor
Alison Goldingham

Designers
Jane Moody Tony De Saulles David Ganderton Lois Wigens

Typeset in Goudy Old Style on Scantext by Thames Head Limited
Reproduction by TPS, Cardiff, Great Britain
Printed in Italy by Arnoldo Mondadori Company Limited

Sneyd, Barbara
Riding high, 1896-1903 : scenes from a lakeland childhood.
1. Lake District (England) — History
I. Title II. Barstow, Phyllida
942.7'8081'0924 DA670.L1

ISBN 0 7207-1711-6

Contents

Introduction 6 – 9

1896 10 – 13

1897 14 – 43

1898 44 – 90

1899 91 – 125

1900 126 – 141

1901–1903 142 – 157

The Epilogue 158 – 159

pansies and forgetmenots
from my garden

wild roses
crimson and white

Introduction

Barbara Sneyd grew up in the last years of Queen Victoria's reign. Her family was then living at Finsthwaite, a handsome Georgian house near the southern end of Lake Windermere which her father, General Thomas Sneyd of The Queen's Dragoon Guards — 'The Bays' — had rented from the Vicar of Staveley. An attractive energetic girl with a lively sense of fun, Barbara showed artistic talent from an early age. Unlike their brother Humphrey, who was sent to boarding school at Sandroyd and later Wellington College, Barbara and her younger sister Idonia were taught at home by governesses. Mrs Sneyd encouraged them to keep diaries: Barbara's took the form of a sketchbook in which she recorded the family's activities, their horses, pets, flowers and any scene that caught her fancy.

Secure in the idyllic countryside of the Lake District, into which neither traffic nor strangers had yet penetrated, the Sneyd children were allowed plenty of freedom. They fished and sailed and swam, shot rabbits and roamed the fells. Despite the hampering clothes of the period — long skirts and buttoned boots, close-fitting jackets and the inevitable hat — the girls took long walks in all weathers and spent much of their time out of doors.

Barbara Sneyd

Barbara rode well and had a quick eye for the funny side of life with horses. Mounted side-saddle on the redoubtable Whalebone, she covered long distances to visit friends or carry messages. Her particular friend and confidante was her cousin Mabel Gale, two years her senior, who lived ten miles away at Bardsea Hall.

In winter Barbara hunted with the Windermere Harriers in the flat, well-fenced country round Cark, or further afield with the Vale of Lune Foxhounds.

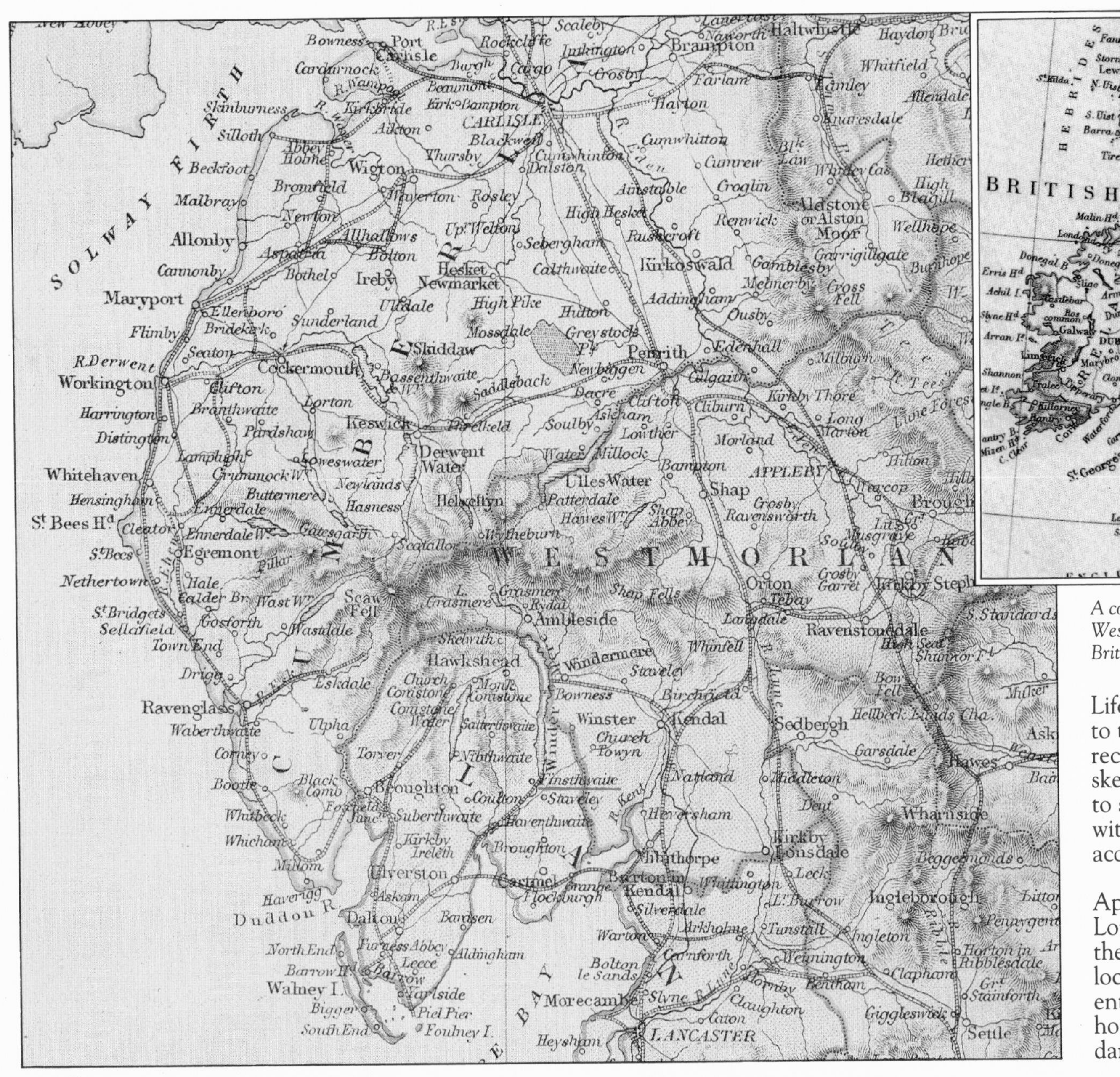

A contemporary map showing the Westmorland and Cumbria area of the British Isles

Life was not all roses. Ten visits to the dentist in Lancaster are recorded in 1897 alone, and sketches of the metal plate used to straighten her teeth bear witness to an uncomfortable acquaintance.

Apart from visits to friends in London, Surrey and Cheshire, the family's interests centred on local society and their entertainments were largely home-made. Fancy dress balls, dances, tableaux and reel parties took place in the big houses of the district around Christmas, and during the summer there were picnics on the lake, archery competitions and tennis parties as well as the family's annual visit to the seaside at Seascale, where a nuclear processing plant now dominates the coastline.

Botany was one of Barbara's greatest interests. She took a keen interest in the changing seasons, picking and drawing wild flowers from the surrounding coppice woods as well as those from her own corner of the walled flower garden. At the age of nineteen she was accepted by the Slade School of Art, to study under Henry Tonks.

It must have been easy to suppose that unruffled life in the Lake District would never change, but the outbreak of the Boer War in 1899 brought the first chill breath from the outside world as boys whom Barbara had known from childhood hurried away to fight in a conflict from which many would not return.

The sketchbooks begin in 1896, when Barbara was fourteen years old, Humphrey twelve and Idonia ten.

The Family

Major-General Thomas Sneyd

Charlotte Sneyd, *his wife*

Barbara, *born 1882*

Humphrey, *born 1884*

Idonia, *born 1886*

Cousin Bee — *Charlotte's cousin, a frequent visitor to Finsthwaite*

Mabel Gale — *Barbara's cousin and confidante*

Lady Sherbrooke — *Charlotte Sneyd's sister*

Servants

Miss Mackenzie — *governess to Barbara and Idonia*

Jones — *groom*

Eva and Sarah — *nursemaids*

Friends

The Tollers — *'Tollie' — Mrs Toller; 'HBT' — her son; a Cheshire family with whom the Sneyds often exchanged visits*

The Schillings — *London friends*

The Townleys — *neighbours on Lake Windermere whose nephew Edmund James married Idonia*

The Rankins, Harrisons, Wilmots — *neighbours*

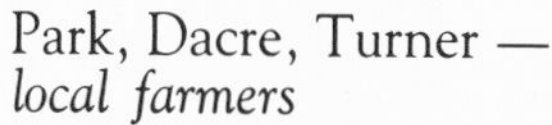

Park, Dacre, Turner — *local farmers*

Miss Harding — *dancing class teacher*

The Animals

Punch
Pixie
The ducks
Whalebone
Major
Spider
Barabbas
Ladas
The ferret
Brunette

Summer 1896

To Mabel Gale, Bardsea Hall

Such drama! Miss Nelson has left us, 'under a cloud,' Eva said, but when I asked what she meant she laughed and wouldn't tell me. She can be very provoking.

It began when Mrs Jones came to the house and asked to speak to Mother. I stood near the door and heard her say, 'It's her or me, Madam;' then Eva made me come away.

Mother told me I could start my summer holiday early as Miss Nelson was leaving. In the autumn she will find me another governess. Poor Miss Nelson! Her eyes were red when I drove her to the station but she said it was the wind. Jones didn't wave goodbye when we passed the stables which I thought strange since they were such good friends and always laughing together.

I went with Mother to Blea Tarn and had a lovely week though she made me learn a poem every day to make up for missing lessons. She hired a fat white pony for me from the farm at Dungeon Ghyll, and he carried me to the top of the fell most pluckily, puffing like a grampus. When I dismounted to admire the view, he flung himself down and rolled on his saddle but I got him up before he broke the tree.

We tried to catch trout but failed miserably and were ourselves devoured by midges. One morning I watched Mr Pickering shearing and he taught me how to score sheep. (You would call it counting.) It goes: Yan, Tyan, Tethera, Methera, Pimp, Sethera, Lethera, Hovera, Dovera, Dick.

Jumping the Hotel proprietors young horse

The departure from Blea Tarn.

The hotel proprietor asked me to try his young horse, so I jumped him in the schooling ground behind the stables. I think the owner hoped we would buy him but he roared like a train so these hopes were soon dashed.

We left after a week in a tremendous thunderstorm and were nearly drowned on our way to the station.

Park has started haymaking in the Big Field and let me help him build haycocks. Mother and Cousin Bee brought a picnic tea, and Idonia tried to hide herself in a heap of hay but left one foot sticking out so we had to pretend we didn't know where she was hiding. At tea she refused to drink her lemonade because two wasps had drowned in it.

Daddy and Humphrey have gone to visit Cousin Ralph Sneyd at Keele. They are coming home on Wednesday.

Carrying the hay in the big field July 1896

Autumn

To Mabel Gale, September

The day before Humphrey went back to school, Daddy took us shooting on the bank below the Tower. I got a rabbit first shot and Humphrey missed two. Jones showed me how to skin my prize, which was interesting if not entirely agreeable.

First you chop off the legs at the hock with a very sharp knife, then slit the skin underneath with great care and loosen it across the back. Next you peel off each hind leg like a tight glove and at last pull the whole skin over the rabbit's head. The smell is awful and clings to your fingers no matter how much you wash.

I am sorry I can't ride over this week, but Idonia is ill with Scarlet Fever and I am not allowed to see anyone. She looks a sorry sight, covered with red blotches, and they have shaved her head. The doctor says it may affect her eyes unless great care is taken to keep her in the dark, so the curtains in her room are drawn all day long.

The Misses Burton have offered to take me in to avoid infection and I am to do lessons with Miss Ada. They have two lovely fluffy cats called Fairy and The Shah, because they are Persian...

Idonia gets scarlet fever and the Miss Burton took me in.

To Mabel Gale, November

...Thank you for your letter. I am glad to be home at last and Idonia is better, though she stays in bed most of the day and whines if I won't play with her. She has become very demanding since she was ill. Eva calls her a Proper Madam.

Daddy and Mother took me to stay with Aunt Carrie at Sherbrooke. We visited the Old Surrey Kennels where the hounds set up a great howl on seeing us — can you wonder! The smell was tremendous. I thought I would choke.

Hounds were meeting at Cross Green, and Aunt Carrie lent me Edward's bay mare. We had a very good day. The country is rather flat, but there are plenty of ditches which my mare jumped grandly.

We stayed in London a few days and Aunt Carrie took me to the Museum of Natural History. I liked the dinosaurs best. Then we went by train to Aston Bank to stay with Mr and Mrs Toller. You would have laughed to see the antics of HBT's pony when Ruby, the groom, tried to clip him. He gave a splendid imitation of a kangaroo and did everything except stand on his head. It took three lads to hold him and at the end the clip was still quite ragged.

Old Surrey kennels

I had a day with the Cheshire Harriers, riding Barabbas. He is the best hunter I have ever ridden, but Tollie would not dream of parting with him. She gave me a cat called Mittens to take home for Idonia. We put her in a basket, but while I was reading the lid popped open. Mittens thought she had spied a mouse lurking under the opposite seat, so decided to travel the rest of the journey on my knee in the hope of catching it.

Today Idonia came downstairs after tea for the first time. She wore a lace veil over her poor shaven head to keep off the draughts, and was so weak and wobbly that Eva and Cousin Bee went one either side of her in case she fell.

February 1897

To Humphrey, Sandroyd School

...I hope you are well and they are not starving you. I rode over to Rusland to choose one of Ruby's pups. They are such beauties and already have quite a look of Sherry, although Mother hopes they will not grow so big. I went to the pen and called them, and chose the one that ran to me first. We have named him Bran after the famous dog of Irish legend.

Mother has decided that I should go on doing lessons with Miss Ada Burton until she finds me a new governess. I hope it will take a long time. Compared to Miss Nelson, Miss Ada is a very easy teacher. After lunch she likes to take a nap, so sets me verbs or tables, but I spend the time much more agreeably drawing horses and flowers in my rough book.

I enclose some little drawings to show you how Pixie amused himself yesterday after escaping from his stall. He scuttled down the drive and into the open gate of Park's meadow where he bucked himself right out of his rug...

Ruby and her pups Jan 1897

To Mabel Gale

...Since I have really outgrown Pixie, Daddy took me to Kendal Fair to look for a horse. It was held near the racetrack just outside the town on a bit of rough ground and you never saw such a scene: horses of all shapes and sizes bucketing back and forth to show their paces, red-faced beery-looking drovers, gypsies with gold ear-rings, mongrel dogs, dealers from the shires, crafty-eyed dealers, donkeys, mountain ponies, newly-weaned foals neighing piteously, and to crown it all a hurdy-gurdy playing 'Drops O' Brandy'. You could hardy hear yourself speak.

We pushed through the crowd and found a few dealers whom Daddy said he could trust. They showed us a strange assortment of horses, some too young, some fit only for the knacker, one with curby hocks, another with windgalls like cushions, yet another which stood so far over at the knee it was a wonder he could even trot, let alone gallop. (Of course, the dealer assured Daddy the ' 'oss 'ad a splendid splendid haction'.)

At last we found a nice dark-brown mare, fifteen hands and six years old, whom I have named Brunette. She is the gentlest creature imaginable and Daddy said she was cheap at thirty pounds.

I will bring her over next week for you to see...

Spring

To Mabel Gale, April

...I am very glad you like Brunette. It is wonderful to ride a bigger horse, though there are perils for anyone kind enough to throw me up — Cousin Bee is still nursing her nose which got in the way of my boot.

Our new puppy has arrived and begun to learn his lessons. Punch showed him how to dig out baby rabbits and swallow them down like oysters, and Mittens warned him to give cats a wide berth.

Daddy, Mother and I went to Liverpool for the Grand National. We walked to the Canal Turn and had a grand view of flying mud and thundering hoofs. It sounded like the roar of the sea as they came past us. The crowd was too thick for us to see anything of the finish, but it was won by Manifesto and all his supporters gave him a great cheer.

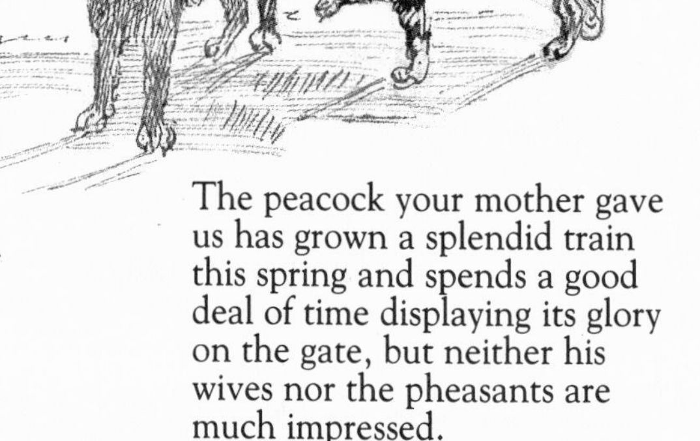

The peacock your mother gave us has grown a splendid train this spring and spends a good deal of time displaying its glory on the gate, but neither his wives nor the pheasants are much impressed.

Next week we start our holiday in Italy. We will visit Venice and Florence...

Pixie & Judas April 1897
Picture for the Lancaster Exibition
chain harrowing the small field.
pen
April 18
A bit of My bed April 1897
The Hermit by Carth
April 1897 by Beadsma

Now we are home again. Humphrey has gone back to school. Jones has got lumbago and Eva has got the toothache and Barbara has gone to Doctor Carmichael to ask if it would be worth while to have her jaw pulled out...

From Idonia's diary

...We are in Italy now, it is covered in snow. Just before we got in the train two men came in and jabbered Italian. They are people who talk nearly the whole time. The trees are cut off so that it leaves a round ball at the top.

We have seen some old ruins on very high mountains. We saw a lovely church with mosaic pictures. We went to the Doge's palace, it was lovely.

We went to see glass being made. They put it in the furnace until it is quite soft, and then he got pincers and pinched it into the shape he wanted. Aunt Carrie gave me a green glass bottle.

The Coach horses

si signorina
April 8th 1897
April 1897
17 April
NORBURY SQUIRE,
Champion hackney
veterinary exam of
April 14th 1897
DIAMOND Jubilee June
1897

Summer

To Mabel Gale

...I am sorry I shan't be able to ride over and see you this week, but I have to go to the dentist's again. Last time Idonia had two stopped, and howled a good deal. I had two pulled out and enjoyed it very much!

To Mabel Gale

...Another visit to the torture-chair. Came back with my face in a pocket-handkerchief...

To Mabel Gale

...Holidays at last! Humphrey came home on Thursday and Idonia and I flung down our pens and embarked on nine weeks' freedom from stuffing in the schoolroom. The very first day we went up to the Tarn and paddled, had our dinner and tea on the Island, then fished the evening rise and caught twenty perch. A record! The water was so clear you could see them take the hook.

Maimie Harrison has asked me to be her bridesmaid, which is so great an honour that I daren't voice any objection to wearing the terrible hat she has chosen. It is just like a tea-tray; Idonia nearly cracked when she saw me try it on.

Daddy came with me to Lancaster about my teeth. He was invited to the luncheon which Lord Derby gave for the High Sheriff and Lord Mayor, and I went with him. In the morning we consulted Mr Cardwell, but it wasn't as bad as before. They gave me a fine mouthful of metal, but had the courtesy to leave my remaining teeth in place. Better still, Mr Cardwell doesn't wish to see me again until October. I can hardly believe my luck.

Afterwards we went in the procession to the Castle. The luncheon was in the Castle grounds, delicious lobster and chicken and strawberry ice, but I left my wine which tasted very sharp.

When we had finished eating there were speeches. The High Sheriff, who seconded the Mayor's vote of thanks to the Earl, constantly referred to 'the Keaunty Taown of Lancashire'. I hid my smiles in my handkerchief!

Yesterday Humphrey beat the family record by eating one hundred gooseberries. Idonia was second with fifty-two. Thanks to my new plate I could only manage twenty-six. Afterwards H looked very green.

August

To Mabel Gale

...Such a calamity, Brunette broke down after a gallop and Mr Aysgill the vet doubts if she will ever be sound enough to ride again, although there is no reason we should not breed from her next year. She was such a sweet mare; if only I hadn't gone so fast! It happened just at the end of the long hill to Rusland. She had been going well and pulling quite hard, then suddenly she staggered and pulled up dead lame behind. I got off and walked her home, but the damage was done. Mr Aysgill says a hind leg is more serious than a foreleg, because it takes so much weight and can't be rested. Jones talked of firing her, but Mr A said it would do no good.

Daddy has got me a new horse on trial from Grange Farm, dark brown with a crooked blaze, very striking. He has such a tough, devil-may-care look about him that I call him Whalebone and hope he lives up to his name.

The first ride I went on him, my stirrup broke. I could not get off to pick it up, so left it lying in the road and bumped home unsupported. Fortunately Whalebone behaved like a perfect gentleman.

Jerry Marriott and his sister Muriel are staying with Cousin Ada Marriott as guests of Mrs Townley at Townhead. On August 14th after the grouse season opened, Daddy, Jerry, Humphrey and I went in search of some for the pot, but they proved hard to find. However, as we went over the moor I spotted a good deal of white heather, so didn't return empty-handed.

my stirrup left me so I left it lying on the road and went on

Tuesday Aug 10th 1897

Daddy, Jerry, Humphrey and self look for grouse. August 14th 1897

One afternoon while I was riding, Humphrey and Idonia persuaded Eva to let them take their tea on the Lake. Unfortunately none of them is an accomplished boatman and when the wind got up they smashed an oar by running against a rock. They had to pay Kellett five shillings, which made a hole in their pocket-money for the week.

Jerry wanted to see Esthwaite Water, so he and I took a long walk over the hill, returning by the Tower and slithering and sliding over loose stones down the steep bank behind the Ferry Hotel. He talked all the way there and all the way back. He can imitate his commanding officer to perfection, and made me laugh very much by recounting some of the stories he heard in the Officers' Mess. Unfortunately he said the best of them were not suitable for the ears of a lady...

To Mabel Gale

...Summer colds are the worst of all. It seems so unfair to be afflicted with a red nose and streaming eyes while the sun is shining. I hope you are already feeling better.

Jerry and Muriel went on to Scotland with Cousin Ada, though we all urged them to spend another week. Muriel's sketches are fine, and Jerry keeps everyone laughing.

Whalebone hasn't the best of feet and has been giving me a good deal of bother. First he kicked off a shoe in the night. I rode him to Newby Bridge for a new one, then made a circuit over the moors behind Field Broughton where the woodcutters are carting timber. Two days later, would you believe, he pulled off the same shoe again. I took him back to the forge, where the smith said if he loses it a third time there won't be enough hoof left to get a nail in. Riding to Ulverston with Olga next day I was very careful to avoid ground that looked boggy and got home safe and sound with all shoes in place.

Miss Burton has given Idonia a new kitten, since Mittens has become so sedate she scorns to play. The newcomer is a fluffy little tabby, such a darling. Idonia lets it sleep in her hat and is hard at work making a purple silk waistcoat which she hopes to persuade Tabby to wear...

1897
Idonia's kitten sleeping in her hat 25th August
August 30th
Daddy and H went out shooting. Mother and
Bee went out calling I stopped at home as
Olga wa coming. she didnt
turn up so I saddled W
and rode out
1897
Olga came in
the pouring rain
and we went to
look for white
heather and got very
wet
28th August
1897
25th Aug 1897
Idonia doing
her sketch
for the club

September

To Mabel Gale

We are all pleased to be back at Seascale, where nothing changes from year to year. Even the bulls-eyes in the sweetshop look exactly the same as the one I broke my tooth on last summer.

When we arrived on Saturday it was blowing a gale. Humphrey and I bathed in the afternoon after persuading Mother to overrule Eva's law that no one should swim on their first day at the seaside. What nonsense! In fact she was almost proved right because the sea was extremely rough and we nearly as possible drowned.

On Sunday it was still very blustery. After Church Idonia took Mother's umbrella to put it up, but the wind caught it and Idonia was blown away down

Sept 11th 1897

6th of Septem 1897 Seascale

H hired a bicycle and collided by himself in less than an hour

After searching all over Seascale for a cob to ride I find an awful hog maned white pony and a minute saddle that ran into me fearfully September 7th 1897

H and Idonia paddling at Seascale Sept 7th 1897

the Promenade with us all in hot pursuit. Mother and I went to a concert at the hotel and heard Mr Rawlinson and Miss E. Fell play their 'cellos quite beautifully.

At low tide Humphrey and I decided to build a huge sand-castle and were soon joined by a boy called Henry who had a proper garden spade. We dug furiously until the castle was three feet high and wide enough for us all to stand on. I made turrets round the top. After supper Mother let us go out and stand on our castle until the tide came right past and we were surrounded by water. In the morning there was not a trace left.

21st Sept 1897 Mother and I and some of the girls went to the Archery on Prize day, Mr Billinge won the cup and Mrs Clarke a silver kettle

After searching all over Seascale for a cob to ride, I found a white pony with an awful hogged mane and a *minute* saddle that ran into me fearfully. His paces were far from comfortable, poor beast, but I thought it better than bicycling. Humphrey, who mastered the technique in less than an hour, preferred his wobbly wheels.

One morning I rode with Miss Kerr, who cut a dashing figure on Robinson's pony in a harness bridle with blinkers!

We will stay here for a fortnight, but I look forward to joining you at the Archery Competition at Greenodd on the 21st.

Daddy heard yesterday that Jerry has been gazetted in the 49th Berkshire, 1st Battalion. He has to join his regiment in the West Indies, embarking on November 1st...

From Idonia's diary

September 5th 1897

It was very rough on the sea and awfully windy when we got here. I was nearly blown away. Humphrey paddled in the morning with me on his back because Eva said I couldn't paddle, and in the afternoon Humphrey was taught to bicycle and could go by himself in an hour.

September 8th

In the morning I paddled a long while, and in the afternoon I tried on a bicycle. It was rather too big for me and it didn't matter which way I leant and guided it, it always leant towards Eva.

September 12th

In the morning Eva and Barbara and Humphrey bathed, and a very big wave came when they weren't looking. In the afternoon Mother and Daddy were having their lunch when Mother felt something moving in her petticoats and she shook them and a mouse came down...

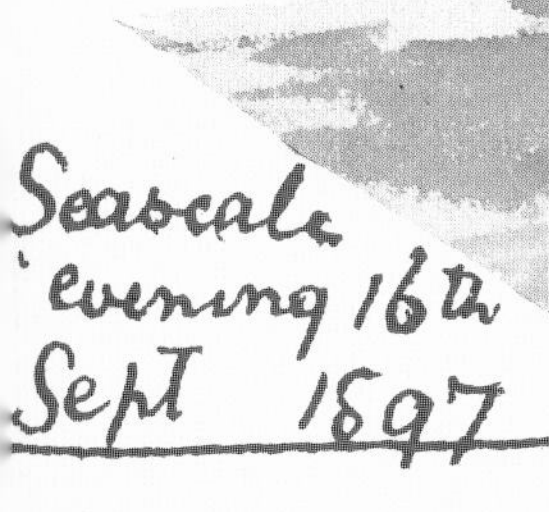

Autumn

To Humphrey, Sandroyd School

...My new governess has come — our new governess, I should say, for she is to teach Idonia as well. Her name is Miss Emily Mackenzie, she comes from Edinburgh and has dark hair in a bun, a strong Scottish jaw, and looks as if she would stand no nonsense.

I heard her tell Mother she believed in plenty of fresh air and exercise for the Growing Girl. Before lessons she makes us do Deep Breathing on the terrace, then I whirl Indian clubs while Idonia skips Salt, Mustard, Vinegar, Pepper until we are both ready to drop! Her system of education is rather different from Miss Nelson's or Miss Ada's. She made me do tests in every subject to find out my standard, and awarded me A for Drawing, English, and Nature; B for History and Geography; C for Latin, and D for horrible Mathematics.

After lessons yesterday Miss Mackenzie walked with us down to Newby Bridge where Mrs Wren let us help to fill the mailbags with her little shovel. It was a beautiful evening so Miss Mackenzie and I climbed up to the Tarn the steep way and did a sketch of the sunset. She draws awfully well and is more energetic than Miss Nelson.

When I asked if she found it steep she said it was nothing compared to the Scottish hills.

We all had a grand time decorating the Church for Harvest Thanksgiving. Miss Mackenzie climbed a ladder to twine garlands round the pillars and I put Park's oat-sheaves round the base. Mother made a beautiful arrangement of flowers and leaves for the altar, and Idonia built stacks of shiny red apples on the ledges below the windows.

"Sunset" on the road to Backbarrow 6th October 1897

Pixie's cart was empty going back, so I gave Bran a ride but he didn't care for it. He leaned so far over the shafts I was afraid he would topple out and whined so much that in the end I let him out to run behind.

On Saturday Daddy went shooting on Colonel Ainsworth's land. They had an excellent day and got thirty-five pheasants.

October

To Mabel Gale

...I had an adventure on my way back from dancing class where I had distinguished myself as usual under the gimlet eye of Miss Harding. I heard the clatter of hoofs behind me, and a cab horse of Robinson's came tearing past, having escaped from his stable.

Whalebone and I set off in pursuit and followed him all the way past the mill and up the steep lane towards Rusland before I managed to lean over and catch his mane. I took one of Whalebone's reins and looped it round the truant's neck.

Miss Harding's dancing class Oct 9th 1897

When I took him down to the forge at Newby Bridge my hat blew off, and before I could turn round to pick it up John Long's dog took a fancy to it and carried it off into the woods to destroy at his leisure. I had to ride home with my head tied up in a handkerchief.

Ladas has grown such a heavy coat that Daddy said he must be clipped to prevent him taking a chill after work. It took Jones four hours, but Ladas stood very well, unlike HBT's pony.

Having once dismounted I was in a quandary, with two horses to lead and no one in sight. (There never is on these occasions.) I managed to hobble as far as Park's farmyard with both horses nipping one another and treading on my heels, and left Robinson's nag there to await collection by his owner. I made sure to shut the top half of the stable door to prevent his breaking out again. Whalebone behaved very well in these trying circumstances, though unfortunately he lost a shoe again.

So I rode home with my head tied up in a pockethandkerchief

My hat blew off and before I could turn round to pick it up John Long's dog carried it off on into the woods--- Oct 13th 1897

Every week Miss Harding devises new horrors at dancing class. This morning she made us throw balls in time to the music but everyone threw at different speeds so the effect was hardly rhythmical. I enjoyed the afternoon a good deal more when I took Whalebone a trial gallop to Rowdsey. He is really fit now and would hardly have blown out a candle when I pulled him up. I shall take him to the Opening Meet on November 3rd

Miss Mackenzie is teaching me the piano. Awful sounds arise from the schoolroom at two-thirty daily...

clipped-Ladas October 14th 1897

driving back from a teaparty at Egton Oct 12th 1897.

To Humphrey, Sandroyd School
October

...I am sorry to hear you have been in the Sick Bay and hope you soon get rid of your spots.

Idonia has started to ride Pixie. Jones takes her out on the leading-rein nearly every day, but when I took her Pixie was very naughty, bucked and shied, and of course Idonia tumbled off, bawling out that she was 'Tewwibly injured!' In fact she was not hurt in the least, only scared, and I made her get on again at once so she wouldn't lose her nerve.

Eva has gone to her new situation and we have a new maid. She comes from Ulverston, has curly dark hair and a big nose and is called Sarah.

Daddy went to Abbotsreading and had a great day — one hundred and fifty pheasants. He took both Punch and Bran and said they were very useful at putting up birds though Bran is still a trifle wild.

Mother took me to the concert at the Jubilee Institute last Saturday where a number of familiar figures appeared on the stage. Mr Kemble sang, 'Come into the Garden, Maud', and Miss Bigland obliged with, 'Love, Let Me Dream Again'. She clasped her hands to her bosom as if squeezing out the highest notes and made soulful eyes. She was much applauded. As the *pièce de résistance* Mr Walker gave his famous recitation in *broadest* Lancashire!

After so much rain, the water is high in the Leven and tomorrow Daddy is going salmon fishing...

Daddy went shooting to Abbotsreading, they shot 150 phea 4 woodcocks.

Mother Miss Mackensie and I went to a concert at the Jubilee Institute October 22nd 1897

come into the garden Maud

Oct 27th A misty afternoon at Grange gulls feeding on the wet sand

To Mabel Gale

...Back to the torture chamber — my tenth visit this year. Miss Mackenzie came with me to Lancaster and listened with a disapproving expression to the ecstasies of the dentists as they reviewed their work. Afterwards she called me a 'puir bairrn' and gave me a lemon ice.

Yesterday there was a sharp frost, so Idonia and I decided it was time Pixie had a good bed. I cut a lot of bracken and heaped it up, then we put string round the whole bundle and pulled it back to the house. It was hard work. When we had bedded down the stable it looked so nice that Pixie would hardly believe it was meant for him.

fleeing from the scarlet fever microbes

29th Oct

I began to read. "The horse in art and nature" by Cecil Brown

Miss M listening to the ecstacies of the dentists over their work Oct 27th at Lancaster – 1897

We all go to a Cinematograph Entertainment at the Swan Hotel Newby Bridge Oct 28

beastly dancing class) Spanish skirt dancing
30th Oct

Mother took all of us to a cinematograph entertainment at the Swan Hotel. The maids went first. We saw living pictures of the Jubilee Procession in London and all the shops. When we came out it was quite dark.

I am reading *The Horse in Art and Nature* by Cecil Brown and find it most illuminating.

Nov 1st 1897 Idonia riding on a jersey calf and Mr Inman fishing

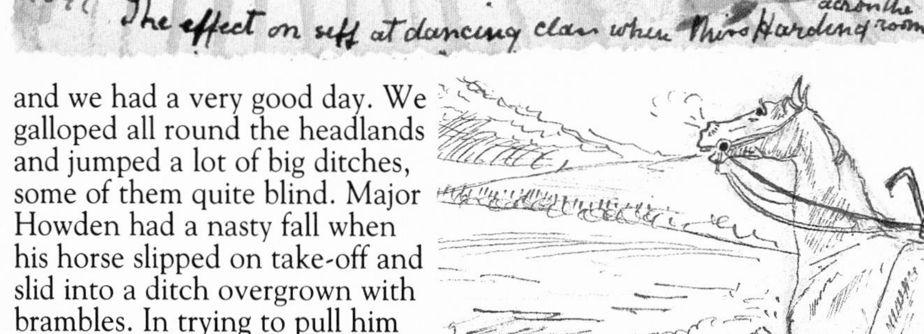

6th Nov 1897 The effect on self at dancing class when Miss Harding remarked on my manner of walking across the room

November

To Mabel Gale

...Since I last wrote I have been hunting twice on Whalebone. He is the best horse I have ever hunted — better even than dear old Barabbas. The Windermere Harriers had their Opening Meet at Newton on November 3rd. When Whalebone heard them some distance away he flung his head high and trumpeted his delight. There were over thirty people out but scent was poor and we had only a few jumps.

The following week the Windermere met at Cark. I took Whalebone there on the train and we had a very good day. We galloped all round the headlands and jumped a lot of big ditches, some of them quite blind. Major Howden had a nasty fall when his horse slipped on take-off and slid into a ditch overgrown with brambles. In trying to pull him out we pulled off his bridle and when at last he scrambled clear he galloped off to join hounds and made a real nuisance of himself. Major Howden broke his collarbone.

boxing hunter for Cark 10th Nov 1897

Whalebone's delight at hearing the Windermere harriers.

Idonia is becoming almost too confident a rider. When we were out for a walk by the river, she

quietly climbed on the back of a Jersey heifer which was lying chewing the cud. It jumped up in a fright, but Idonia clung on to it until Miss Mackenzie told her to jump off at once.

You are lucky Cousin Helen doesn't make you go to dancing class. This is the effect Miss Harding produces on my complexion when she remarks on my manner of walking! We are learning a new dance in which we whirl flounced skirts to and fro like chorus girls. Violet H takes care to place herself near the front of the class where she will catch Miss Harding's eye.

While out riding the other morning I saw the most comical punting accident at Abbotsreading. The water-meadows were flooded and Idi and George Rathbone had fashioned a rather unseaworthy raft out of planks and casks which they were rowing about when it upset and they both fell in the water.

I decided to have Whalebone clipped but Jones was busy so I did it myself and feel quite proud of the result. Removing his whiskers has greatly improved the appearance of his head and he doesn't take half so long to dry off after work.

Winter

To Humphrey, Sandroyd School
December

...Congratulations on getting your Colours! Daddy is very pleased: I heard him telling Colonel Harrison when they were shooting.

Last week Daddy's new hearing aid arrived. It seems to work pretty well. No longer does the breakfast table echo to cries of 'What? Speak up! Don't mumble.' Instead he begs us not to shout at him!

Doctor Carmichael gave a Magic Lantern show in our schoolroom and lectured us on the subject of 'Our Metropolis.' He had some beautiful clear slides of the Tower of London and of Westminster Abbey among other places. Quite a lot of people came and we brought chairs from all over the house. Mrs Townley brought Mr Townley's nephew from America. His name is Edmund James, he is eleven years old and comes from Red Willow County, Nebraska. Miss Mackenzie made us look it up in the big Atlas to see where it was. He is to live at Townhead, since Mr and Mrs Townley have no children, but I think he misses his family a lot. He looked very lonely. At first he was shy and would hardly speak, but Idonia showed him her kitten and soon put him at ease with her chatter.

The weather here is wild, wet and windy...

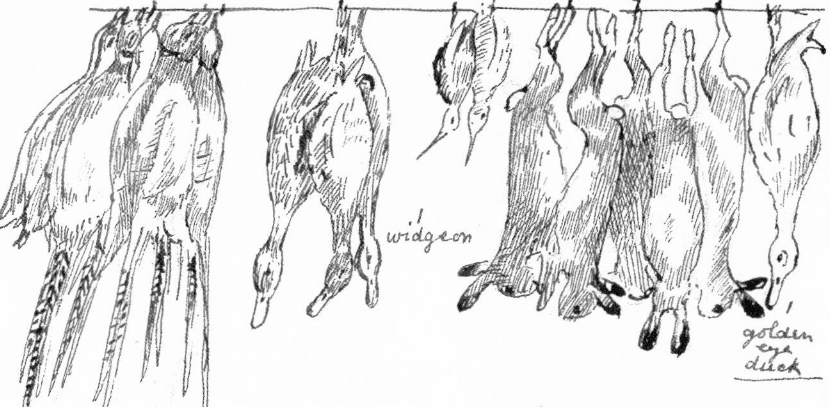

Our game larder
Nov 1897

To Mabel Gale

...Such a day we had from Cark! I must tell you about it. Daddy lent Ladas to Colonel Wilmot, and we put the horses on the train and arrived at Cark station in good time. Whalebone was very excited, star-gazing and jogging, and gave me quite an uncomfortable ride to the meet.

Magic lantern at Finsthwaite Schoolroom 25th November 1897
Subject of lecture
"Our Metropolis"

However, he settled down before we reached East Plain and we got there before the hounds did. I counted twenty-five mounted and twice that number of foot-followers.

Two coverts were drawn blank, then we started a hare near Allendale Farm and she ran in a big circle, crossing the flats and the railway line, along the embankment, then across the drainage ditches to Oldmoor, where hounds bowled her over in the open.

Major Wilmot and I were first to come up with them, and only the dealer from Grange and the farrier's son (I don't know his name but he has a good little black pony — a real flier) stayed with us throughout the run. Some more joined us later. Mr Torrance flew one ditch ahead of his horse, which made us all laugh. He always gets in the most unlucky accidents and was much chaffed afterwards for the mud on his fine new coat. Whalebone galloped and jumped like a good 'un.

In the late afternoon we found again and had another fast run but Ladas lost both his front shoes in some plough, so we led him back. When we got to Newby Bridge it was quite dark.

Major Wilmil
and self had a
very good day
with the
Windermere
splendid runs
Cark 1st Decem

December

To Mabel Gale

...It has been such a dreadfully wet week, with the going so muddy that I have kept entirely to the roads for fear of losing Whalebone's shoes.

Ladas does not care for pulling the carriage in such weather and has a decided way of showing his disapproval. When passing Kellett's on the way to the station he took fright at a loose shutter (or pretended to) caught the bit in his teeth and bolted all the way to the village, giving Jones a bad scare.

Ladas bolted from Kellets to the village on the way to the station 16 Dec

Just try this little toque Madam

Cousin Bee took me to Lancaster for my latest visit to the torture-chamber. On the way her eye was attracted to an absurd feathered hat and nothing would do but she must try it on. Five tall plumes in grey and maroon: you can imagine the effect above her long pale face! After a dramatic display of hesitation she bought it for two guineas and bore it home in triumph.

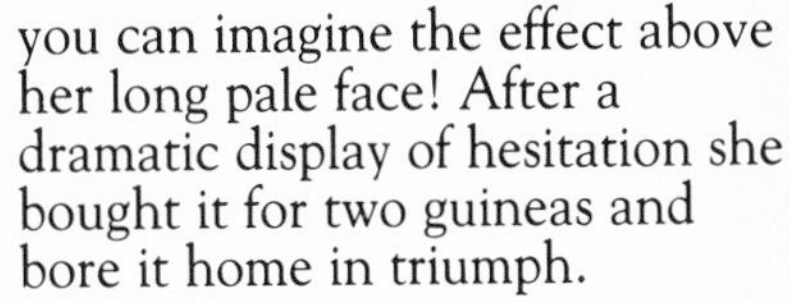

What I look like in the rain 13th

On Friday the Vale of Lune met at Newton, but it poured relentlessly all day long so I didn't go but tried instead to concentrate on my lessons. Vain hope! Hoofs kept galloping over my French précis and Miss Mackenzie chanting Latin verbs became the voice of the huntsman cheering on hounds...

Stormy sunset view from the schoolroom window 8th December

The Vale of Lune met at Newton Friday 17th Dec rained the whole day so didn't go did lessons instead.

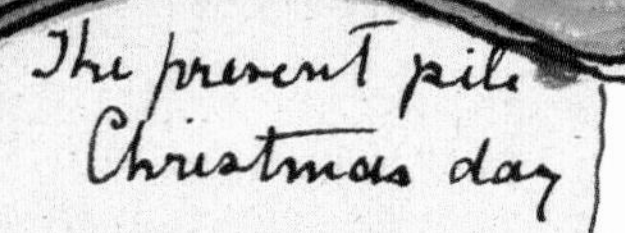

To Mabel Gale

…Miss Mackenzie went to Edinburgh to spend Christmas with her parents and we have begun our holidays. When Humphrey came home, Mother took one look at him and summoned Mr Fizackerley the barber. He draped a sheet about Humphrey's shoulders and snipped away; then he told him to shut his eyes whilst he blew in his face with great violence. Humphrey was somewhat disgusted!

Idonia has made a beetle on a pin as a present for Olga, so I rode over to Haverthwaite to deliver it on Christmas Eve. It was frightfully slippery.

Humphrey made some pastry and ate a good deal of it at tea beside other things, He didnt feel hungry next morning curious to relate.

we went to a party at Egton Vicarage

Whalebone could hardly keep his feet on the hill. When I got back I found Idonia decorating the nursery with the holly we found near Rusland, so I helped her put it up.

All our presents are wrapped and hidden in the hall under a velvet curtain. The mountain seems to grow every time I look at it.

Humphrey pestered Mrs Cook until she let him make some pastry. He ate a good deal of it raw, and more at tea besides other things, and afterwards looked very pale. He didn't feel very hungry next morning, curious to relate.

Jones is going to drive us over to your dance next week. We are looking forward to it very much...

Whalebone and I rode to Haverthwaite with a message it was frightfully slippery 24th Decem 1897

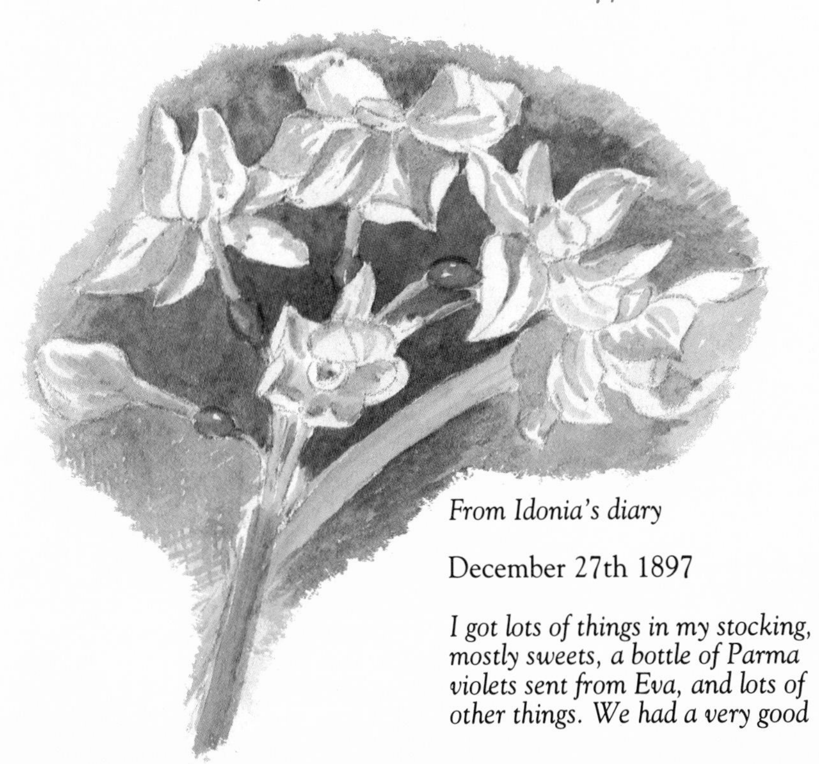

From Idonia's diary

December 27th 1897

I got lots of things in my stocking, mostly sweets, a bottle of Parma violets sent from Eva, and lots of other things. We had a very good dinner of turkey. The doctor gave me a tea-set. The cups are so sweet. I am now playing halma with the red halma set which Sarah bought yesterday.

There was a thunderstorm in the evening. The Gales came over to stay a night because they were going to the Harrisons' dance. It lasted until two o'clock in the morning. Barbara and Humphrey and I are going to a party at the Townleys'. We start at six o'clock and stay until ten. Sarah is going to drive down with us and then going to see her mother. I am going to wear my grand frock...

Humphrey went for a ride with me 1st Jan 1898

coming back from Eglon
New Years eve

January 1898

To Mabel Gale

...Here are some little sketches I made of your Ball. My first grown-up dance, and I enjoyed it all the more when I saw you had asked Jerry. As soon as I saw his funny crooked grin I stopped feeling that my hands were too big and everyone was wondering why I am not a Beauty like Mother.

One burning question: how did you learn to waltz without the benefit of Miss Harding's instruction? You were quite the belle of the ball. After trampling one another's feet for a while, Jerry and I decided to sit out our dances — no doubt he was as thankful as I was! He made me laugh with his imitations of certain people of our acquaintance. When he did Mr Townley I nearly cracked.

We have had such a round of gaiety since Christmas I am quite worn out. First your dance, then the Harrisons' party where we played Blind Man's Buff and reverted to childhood — some of us too far. Idonia made a fearful scene when the Blind

We went to a dance at Bardsea Hall Jan 4th 1898 there were about 60 people

Bardsea Hall Jan 4th
1898

Man captured her and Sarah had to take her away.

Hard on the heels of the Harrisons' came the Stanleys' Reel Party. I only wish I could master the intricacies of Scottish dancing. Maisie tried without much success to instruct us: there was a good deal of pushing and prodding which left me little the wiser.

On Saturday we had a dose of fresh air when Edmund and Stephen Pilkington came to shoot with Daddy. That evening they helped make costumes for Tableaux at the Burtons'. We dressed Jack Deakin as the Tin Soldier, with a splendid bearskin

blind mansbuff at the Harrisons Jan 6th 1898

Tablease at the Burtons 11th Jan. 1898

Now that little tin soldier he puffed with pride, at being marked 2 and 3 and the saucy little dolly girl smiled once more for he'd risen in life d'yo see

made from a rolled hearthrug; Humphrey was the Officer in an old mess jacket of Daddy's — far too big for him, so we stitched the back seam in a huge tuck — and Idonia the saucy Little Dolly Girl. She looked sweet in an old yellow dress of mine with a big satin sash...

From Idonia's diary

January 14th 1898

In the morning it was wet. I stayed in and finished my painting, and pulled Sarah's chair away just as she was going to sit down. The consequences were awful. Barbara is going hunting with Jones. She was very quick about getting up this morning. Mother is marking Humphrey's clothes for Wellington. She made a great many blots...

To Mabel Gale

...I must tell you about my visit to Aston Bank. I felt quite the young lady of fashion setting off on my own, with boxes and trunks enough for a six-month stay rather than six days. Hunting clothes are so very cumbersome to pack, and Mother wanted me to wear my new habit. It was delivered just before Christmas and is so beautiful I am almost afraid to get mud on it.

The train arrived a little early, but as I stood on the platform with my luggage piled around me, wondering how to deal with it, HBT came running towards me, followed by Tollie who soon engaged a pair of porters to stow it in the carriage, and we rattled back in fine style with HBT driving.

Next day he taught me to ride a bicycle by the simple method of telling me not to look at the front wheel. I looked well ahead, pedalled as instructed — and lo and behold I could bicycle! Not a single tumble. Delighted by this success I spent the whole afternoon pedalling round the lanes in HBT's wake, toiling up hills for the pleasure of flying down. It is a glorious feeling.

Tollie lent me Barabbas for a day with the North Cheshire. Though he is now sixteen years old he goes splendidly. I mean no disloyalty to Whalebone when I say Barabbas is a more peaceful ride (though perhaps not so exciting). We met at the Kennels, found in the laurels at the back of them, and hunted what must have been the resident Kennel fox in a big circle, all on good old turf with well-laid fences. There was quite a big Field and I saw some prime examples of horsemanship. One bowler-hatted individual, sitting well back as his horse constantly refused a fence, enquired in sarcastic tones 'if he meant to stop there all day?' while another fat red-faced farmer in leather gaiters had the habit of dismounting before every hedge and forcing his way through backwards, dragging his horse with him. I suppose he found it safer than jumping!

Mr and Mrs Toller had to go to Widnes, so I rode Barabbas a long hack towards Eaton Hall and got myself quite lost, but the clever old fellow knew his way home when I let the reins hang loose. The girls have the sweetest terrier puppy, four months old, with a little stumpy tail and a black, white and tan coat, called Jacko. They hope he will take after his mother who is the star ratter of the Hunt Kennels.

Tollie took me to Liverpool to see the collection of pictures in the City Art Gallery — works by Holbein, Rembrandt and some lovely Impressionists as well as more modern paintings. We had a hazardous crossing of the Mersey in a gale. The steamer was tossed about and the yachts heeled over with their masts almost touching the waves.

Jones made the excuse that he had been too busy to exercise Whalebone properly while I was away. I knew very well he had preferred to stay snug in the tack-room cleaning harness to riding my gallant steed. In consequence Whalebone was very fresh, buckjumped and plunged when I took him for a gallop, and nearly as anything unseated me.

Mr Toller took me to Liverpool to see the collection of pictures. we crossed the Mersey in a steamer, and walked about the docks 29th January 1898

On Tuesday we start lessons again. Cousin Bee has gone to London, and tomorrow Miss Mackenzie is coming back from Scotland by the four o'clock train.

February

From Idonia's diary

February 7th *1898*

After lessons we went for a walk and saw the steam roller. When we turned up towards Newby Bridge we saw Barbara riding. She went for a gallop to show me Whalebone's pace.

February 11th

Today is Barbara's birthday. She got two pairs of gloves and a cotton handkerchief and a silk one. We had lessons morning and afternoon. Miss M let us out a little early because I was going to ride dressed like a boy. It was awfully nice. People seemed to think I was a boy. I had a very massive behind.

The "Windermere" met at
East Plain Cark, 10-30 Feb 16th
Jones and I went it was very windy but
we had a splendid day. Whalebone jumped splendidly
and carried me through two fast runs

jumping under difficulties
my appearance in the first run
an unpleasant catastrophe
in the course of the day a farmers wife lent me a hat and hurriedly tied up my hair in an enormous bow Feb 16 th 1898

To Mabel Gale

...The Windermere met at East Plain, Cark, on Wednesday. Jones and I had a splendid day, although it was very windy. Jones fell off Ladas twice, but Whalebone never put a foot wrong and carried me grandly through two fast runs. As we were approaching a ditch my hat flew off and my hair blew all over my face so I could hardly see. However, in the course of the day a farmer's wife lent me a hat and hurriedly tied up my hair in an enormous bow. Mr Dickinson rode under a low branch and was swept from the saddle like Absalom, and Tom Tidey's mare was kicked by the huntsman's horse when he dismounted to break up the hare. She had a big bump on her knee and was very lame so a few compliments were exchanged between Jem and Tom Tidey!

Next morning Whalebone was a little stiff and so was I, but he trotted up sound...

hound trail 7th Feb 1895

Exercising Whalebone the day after hunting 17th Feb 1895

Ladas the buckjumper

March

snow mountain up the Lake
17th Feb 1898 ——

To Humphrey, Wellington College, Crowthorne, Berks.

...Since you went back I have been shooting three times but failed to get any more rabbits. The dogs are most frustrated. It is clear they think me a rotten shot and long for your return. I saw two black rabbits below the Tower, and a cock and hen pheasant — out of season of course!

Idonia rides nearly every day and when Jones is too busy to go with her she accompanies me on my morning rides. We went to see Knowles's chestnut mare and her new foal. Although there is snow on the hills he still puts them out to grass every day and I must say they do look very well. He says it doesn't do to molly-coddle horses.

On Saturday we went to dancing class at Ulverston, and at the end of the lesson Miss Harding asked me for a waltz. Great honour! Violet Harrison, the Show Dancer of the class, hoped she would be chosen to partner Miss H and her astonishment was comical to behold when the privilege fell upon me.

great honour
Miss Harding
walsed with me
March 19th 1898

Riding through Newby Bridge, I saw people running from their houses in great excitement. 'The motor-car is coming!' was the cry. I pulled Whalebone into a side street just in time before a noisy and excessively smelly horseless carriage drove past us to the amazement of the populace. Whalebone did not care for it at all and I had some difficulty stopping him from bolting. The machine was driven by Major Pickering, with his nephew Tommy beside him.

Tollie has come to stay for a few days. She and I went a lovely long walk by the river on a sunny afternoon and found the first primroses. It must be an early spring, because I picked the first piece of larch on March 15th...

Tollie and I went
a lovely walk by the river and
found some primroses
9th March
1898
Picked the first bit
of larch March
15th 1899
SUNSET AT NEWBY
BRIDGE 13th March

April

To Mabel Gale

...Humphrey is home for Easter and Idonia and I finished lessons the same day. Miss Mackenzie has gone to Edinburgh for a week, but will come back for her examination in Bandaging and First Aid. She practised bandaging on me and Idonia before she left, binding our heads and limbs until we could hardly move and looked like war wounded. Mother came into the schoolroom and had quite a scare.

Last week Whalebone and I were caught in a fearful blizzard while out exercising. It blew up from nowhere. Quite suddenly the blue sky turned dark and then stinging hailstones lashed us with such force that we scuttled for home at a butcher-boy trot. Whalebone's mane and my eyelashes were stiff with ice.

Alas, the hail destroyed most of the lovely blossoms on my peach tree. Only one branch escaped, but the daffodils at Abbotsreading have survived the storm, goodness knows how. Although they look so delicate they must be very tough. Sarah and I picked a great many bunches to send to the hospital, even when we finished the pale yellow carpet seemed untouched.

I have finished the suit of clothing for my model horse 'Lord Grey' and will bring him over to show you. Mother gave me an old ulster of Daddy's to cut up, and I have bound the edges with braid.

Dancing class has finished for the term, thank goodness, and Violet had her moment of glory when she performed the Cinderella Skirt Dance in front of the whole class. I have to admit she did it very well and was heartily applauded.

The Windermere have finished the season, but it is still too cold to turn the horses out so we continue to ride every day. I took Whalebone mountaineering on Stott Park Heights and also over Bigland Hill, taking Bran with me for the exercise, but I had to keep him strictly to heel near Field Broughton, where there was a lovely field of daffodils and young lambs skipping about in them.

Yesterday Mother entertained the Ladies' Working Party, and when they had finished tea they came to admire the huge bonfire which Daddy helped us build on the edge of the wood to burn up the woodcutters' leavings...

May

To Humphrey, Wellington College

...After lessons Idonia and I have been making ourselves useful by riding errands for Mother. We must have covered a dozen miles and saved Jones so much time that he was able to polish the carriage until you could see your face in it. First we went to Backbarrow and ordered corn, then got a five shilling postal order from Newby Bridge for Mother to send for autumn shrubs from a catalogue. On our way back we fetched the newspapers from the station but unfortunately I dropped the copy of the *Lancashire Gazette* just at Pixie's heels. He lashed out with one hind-leg and neatly bisected the newspaper, which didn't improve its reading qualities.

Idonia went out riding with me we went to Backbarrow ordered some corn and got a postal order at Newby Bridge and fetched the newspapers from the Station May 2nd 1895.

cherry tree May 3rd 1895 below the tower

Found a jackdaw's nest. the tower & it was very windy I was in an awful funk that the tower would blow down.

With Ladas between the shafts it took Mother and me only a little over an hour to drive to Bardsea. Mabel showed me her new black mare, Maud — very sleek and breedy. Privately I thought her

Rode pixie bareback down to Newby Bridge with a parcel May 10th

Mabel's black mare "Maud"

Mother and I drove to Bardsea May 7th 1895

a trifle light of bone, though I was tactful enough not to say so to the proud owner.

Yesterday evening I went up to the Tower. You remember where we saw that jackdaw fly out carrying a beakful of twigs? Now there is a nest with four eggs. The wind was so strong that I was in an awful funk that the Tower would blow down, and therefore didn't linger or take an egg. I will write and let you know if they hatch.

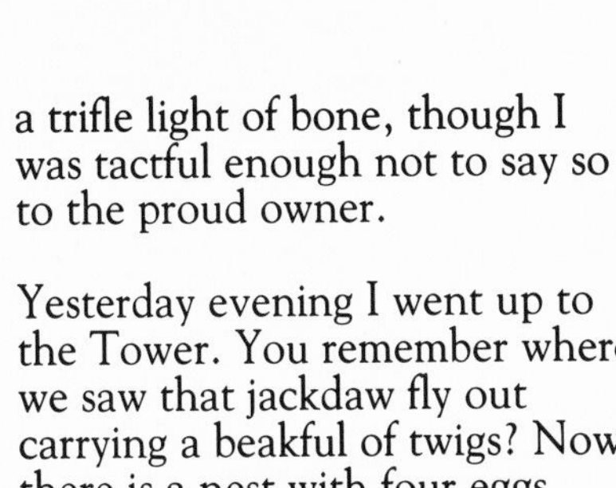

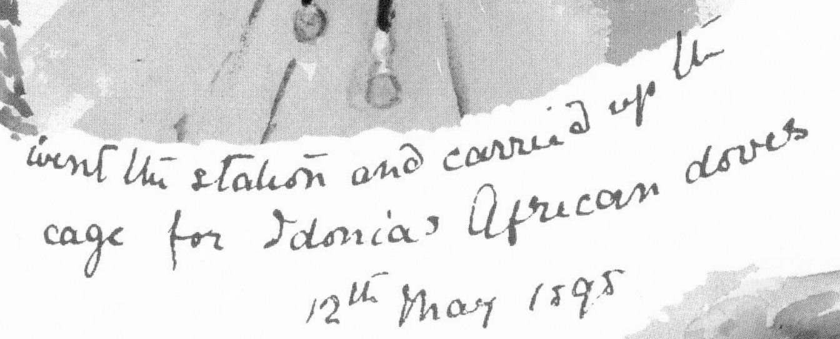

Daddy ordered a new cage from the Army and Navy Stores for Idonia's doves, and as Jones had earache I rode Whalebone to the station and carried it up. It is bigger and altogether better than the old one and has a special nesting compartment, so she hopes they will breed this year.

Tomorrow Whalebone goes out to grass, so Pixie's services will be required...

Lilac June
1898
Topthorn's jockey
seeing to the girths before
the Northern Counties half-bred
Steeplechase May 30th
1898
5th June

Cartmel May 30th 1898

To Mabel Gale

...I meant to ask when we saw you, do you mean to come to Cartmel for the races? I hope so. I rode there yesterday and ordered stables for our horses, and took the opportunity of booking them for you as well. There was an awful crowd at the hotel. I was barely in time to secure the last four stalls...

June

To Mabel Gale, 60 Gloucester Terrace, London

...I hope you are enjoying The Season. On your return I look forward to hearing your advice upon the following:

How to behave in Society

How to converse with Young Men

Ditto with Distinguished Old Buffers

The Gentle Art of Flirtation...and kindred subjects!

My charges out at grass June 6th 1898 Mother and Daddy went up to London and Jones went for his holiday

We have had two glorious weeks, hot and sunny without the least hint of thunder. Mother and Daddy have also gone to London for some parties and Jones is on his holiday, leaving me in sole charge of the horses at grass. They look fat and well, there being no flies yet to bother them. I love to see them dreaming under the chestnut trees, lips sagging, ears flicking, tails lazily swishing, but to Miss Mackenzie who abhors idleness in man or beast, the sight is like a red rag to a bull.

'How can they stand there all day?' she scolds. 'They do nothing from morning till night. They are even too lazy to graze!'

She takes good care Idonia and I are not tempted into the same snare by keeping us usefully employed all day, taking washing to Newby Bridge or fetching the newspapers. In her eyes any activity is better than none — but sometimes I can't help envying the horses.

I & Miss Mackenzie and F drove over to Cartmel for the Choir Festival. 15th June 1898

We drove Miss M over to Cartmel for the Choir Festival. It was a big affair with thirty choirs from all over the country. A lot were from Wales. The final chorus — in which everyone joined — made a splendid din which must have been heard for miles.

On Violet's birthday, Mrs Harrison asked us to a picnic at Blakeholm. We ate jelly, eclairs and a fine chocolate cake at the water's edge, and afterwards played Hide and Seek and Tom Tiddler's Ground. The dogs got very excited and Miss Rankin's terrier snapped at Sarah but fortunately did no damage beyond tearing her skirt.

Two more visits to the torture-chamber this month — when will they ever end? My mouth is so full of metal I can hardly swallow my food but try as I may I can see no difference in my appearance.

The Harrison's picnic on Blakeholm 14th June

On Midsummer Day I rode with Idonia to Newby Bridge to watch the four-in-hands start for Grange Sands. They were guided by an old man who looked somewhat like a heron, with long thin legs and long nose under thick beetling brows. He told me his father and grandfather had been the only men who knew the sands well enough to guide travellers across in safety, and his grandfather had witnessed the disaster long ago — I think he said 1798 — when four coaches, sixteen horses and countless passengers were lost without trace. Seeing that the channels shift daily, I find this easy to believe. Personally I would rather drive round the bay than risk the crossing…

First rose off my tree 24th June
1898
Grange sands on the way to Lancaster 22nd June.
Mrs Simkin
24th June

Idonia and I fished in the
tarn June 30th
began to cut the grass in
27th June
Parks feild
1st Jelly

Gabriel Junks preening himself on the gate 7th July 1895

July

To Humphrey, Wellington College

...I was delighted and so excited to hear of your great innings! What a shame you didn't quite make the century. Better luck next time!

Things go on here pretty much as usual but the weather has turned heavy and thundery. Luckily Park cut a good crop of hay and carried it while it was still fine.

On our last visit to the Tarn Idonia caught seven perch. She was so proud of her skill that she made me row her about all afternoon despite the fact that I wanted to sketch. She and I were invited to tea at Rusland on Wednesday and rode over on Whalebone and Pixie. The horses were quite suspicious of Sheridan, whom they considered altogether too large for a dog. They snorted and stamped and pretended he was a wolf. For two pins Whalebone would have struck out at him.

Fetched the newspapers through swarms of flies and dust 11th July

12th July young swallows just ready to fly from their nest on the portico

Gabriel Junks has become very noisy in the mornings. His wives are nesting in the nettles above the stableyard — Jones thinks they may be sharing a nest because they take it in turns to come to the corn-hopper. Meanwhile Gabriel keeps them informed of local news by perching on the roof and uttering loud blaring honks. It is quite impossible to sleep later than six o'clock.

The flies are so bad now that Jones brings Ladas and Whalebone into the stable after breakfast and only turns them out at dusk. Even so, Ladas has rubbed his mane and tail quite badly. I rode to fetch the newspapers through swarms of flies and dust, and had to beat a branch about my head and Whalebone's to keep them at bay.

The family of young swallows in the portico is already preparing to fly. Miss Mackenzie says they will never touch the earth while they live because their wings are too long for them to take off again if ever they were forced to land. What a story!

Pixie waiting for the Smith 14th July

Tropeolum 17th July 1895

eucalyptus flower from Bardrea Hall

Idonia and I rode over to Ruxland Hall
to tea July 2nd
pansies and forgetmenots
from my garden
July 5th
wild roses
crimson and white

To Mrs Toller, Aston Bank, Cheshire

...Thank you very much for your letter and the ten shillings. Such riches! I have bought new brushes, some water-colours and a sketchpad, as well as *Pen and Pencil Sketches* by H.S.Marks which I find quite absorbing.

Last week we drove over to Bardsea Hall for a tennis party of Mabel's, but I spent most of the afternoon walking round the garden with Cousin Helen. She knows a lot about flowers and let me take some cuttings.

We have a very fine crop of blackcurrants this year. Miss Mackenzie, Sarah and I picked enough for Mrs Cook to make four dozen pots of jam. While we were working, Idonia gorged on fruit until her teeth turned an attractive shade of blue.

Do you remember the old bay mare of Park's whom you said must have good blood in her somewhere? She has a lovely colt foal, born this year. I walked down to Brookfield to introduce him to the delights of sugar-lumps after supper last night, then on my return had an exciting chase after a huge daddy-long-legs which had invaded my room in search of company. The pace was hot but I bowled him over at last...

nemophila

The pigeons 18th July
bog asphodel
Fished in our larn and got waterlilies 23rd July.
23rd July
Idonia gorging in the Blackcurrant Bushes 18th July 1898

August

To Mabel Gale, Hotel de L'Angleterre, Deauville, Normandy, France

...It is too bad not to see you all summer. I suppose Continental travel will have compensations, but consider the pleasures you are missing here!

Our holidays began officially on July 25th, which Miss Mackenzie and I celebrated with a visit to

Miss Fell's Orchestra at a bazaar at Grenodd.

the bazaar at Greenodd. Miss Fell's orchestra played selections from 'The Merry Widow' while we plunged our arms in the bran-tub, threw hoops over sticks and rolled pennies down slides. Somehow they *never* landed precisely in the middle of the square you aimed at, but I did win a coconut with a lucky throw, and Idonia's ticket in the raffle secured her a large jar of fudge, which made the journey home pass very pleasantly!

Mr and Mrs Schilling and their sons Alfred and Peter stayed a week at the Swan Hotel at Newby Bridge. Idonia and I were invited to tea with them, and after we went on the river. Coming back we caught an eel for some men who had lost their line and Freddie, who insisted on rowing though he had never done it before, caught several crabs.

Miss Rankin's dog "Tippoo"

More aquatic amusement when Idonia and I drove over to lunch with the Rankins, and went up the lake in an Electric launch. This excitement proved too much for Miss Rankin's Tippoo (the terrier who bit poor Sarah at the picnic). His heart is quite as black as his namesake's. Spying a passing branch from his station in the bows, he plunged overboard to seize it. Miss Rankin screamed out that he would be drowned (though he could swim perfectly well) and obliged the captain to go about to pick up the little wretch. When he was hauled aboard he delivered the stick to his mistress, then favoured the rest of us with a shower of water.

Humphrey went for a swim in the tarn in the evening August 14th

Idonia and I drove over to lunch with the Rankins and went up the lake in an Electric launch August 1st 1898

Peter Matheson, who is captain of Humphrey's House, came to stay on his way to Scotland. They were both invited to play for Colonel Ross's team in a match at Merlewood, but lingered so long in the billiard-room after luncheon that they missed the train.

waterlilies on Esthwaite Water 17th on the way to Hawkshead.

Consternation! Jones harnessed Pixie in haste, and I drove them over to Grange as fast as he could lay legs to the ground. We got there in just an hour. Humphrey made twenty-six Not Out, and Peter took three wickets, thus upholding the honour of Finsthwaite.

this is how we missed the train for a match at Merlewood.

After Peter had left, Humphrey and I got up at six in the morning to follow the Kendal Otterhounds. They met at Greenodd at 8.15am, and spent a hot morning hunting the Crake up to Lowick Bridge, but killed nothing.

and had to drive over to Grange in about an hour which we just managed.

My bedroom has become a haven of insect life. I am sending you a selection of my more persistent lodgers...

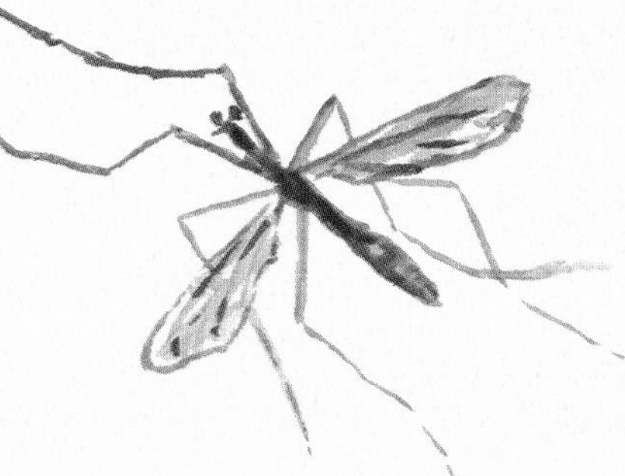

my lodgers August 1895.

Autumn

To Mabel Gale, Bardsea Hall
September

...Only a week left of the summer holidays. It is strange how long they seem at the start and how short at the finish.

Humphrey and I are making the most of our last days of freedom. We went for a picnic with the Wilsons at the Tarn above Hawkridge. It was a steep climb to get there lugging the baskets, and I didn't think it nearly as pretty as our own Tarn (though Mrs Wilson pronounces it 'Perfection!')

Harriet and Mary and I swam while the boys fished from the boat and Idonia paddled at the water's edge. Suddenly we heard a shriek and saw her legs waving frantically: we rushed over and fished her out. Though wet, she was none the worse but Mrs Wilson insisted she should run about to dry off her dress before tea. While thus engaged, she found two adorable mottled toads which we captured and brought home.

Mother has found a big glass bowl for them and they seem quite contented in captivity.

Judging the turnouts

Humphrey and I drove over to Cartmel Agricultural Show Sept 10th 1898

It keeps us all busy catching enough flies to satisfy their appetites. Idonia plagues the life out of the housemaids, making them search behind the pelmets and along the skirting-boards. The house has never been so clean! She is greatly taken with her new pets and loves seeing them flick out their long tongues to transfix their dinner, while their expressions remain perfectly unconcerned.

On Saturday Humphrey and I drove over to Cartmel Agricultural Show, where he made a bee-line for the machinery. The noise and smell of traction engines showing their paces soon drove me away and I spent a more agreeable afternoon watching horses being judged — first hunters, then the turn-outs.

There were more entries than last year in both classes, and the standard was high. I met Mr and Mrs Harrison who invited me to share their tea. No sooner was the lid of the hamper lifted than Humphrey appeared as if by magic, drawn by the magnet of a large fruit cake.

He is going to stay a few days with the Sherbrookes, who have invited him to shoot partridges, lucky fellow! He returns to Wellington the following Tuesday. The Harrisons have asked me to go with them to Ulverston Show next week, where Violet is showing Ozymandias in the Hunter Class, but I believe Mason's young mare from Grange will beat him. I hope to see you before then and hear of your triumphs on the Continent!

October

To Mabel Gale, Bardsea Hall

...On Monday, when Idonia and I started lessons, I learned with some dismay that this will be my last term with Miss Mackenzie. She has persuaded Mother that it would be 'good for me' to be sent away to boarding-school, and says I ought to meet girls of my own age. When I protested I already know lots of girls, she said it would be 'good for me' to get away from home.

Good for me — I ask you! How can it possibly be good for a person to leave all the people (and animals) and the place she loves best, not to mention losing a season's hunting? I shall feel a fish out of water and the prospect fills me with horror.

spent the whole day in the stable sketching for the Competition at Bushey

Whalebone came up from grass Oct 1st 1895

Despite my arguments, Miss M has succeeded in convincing Mother and my appeals to Daddy met with little response. The search has begun for a suitable establishment: Aunt Carrie suggests a school near Windsor called Northlands where the daughters of several of her friends have been educated. Windsor! How can I bear to go so far away? Why can't I stay here where I am happy?

This dark cloud on my horizon has been intensified by this week of the wettest wildest Autumn weather I can remember, and riding is hardly a pleasure. Whalebone came up from grass on October 1st and Jones gave him a physick ball which he swallowed with marked reluctance. I often wonder what good it does. He looked very wretched afterwards, but Jones is set in his ways and won't hear of bringing up a hunter without physicking him.

I spent a whole day last week in the stable, sketching him (Whalebone, not Jones!) for the competition at Bushey. The result was quite satisfactory.

Went to Stott Park in the storm 17th

Dancing class has started. Miss Harding put on her thinking-cap during the summer and devised a new torment called the tambourine dance. I thought it perfectly idiotic but Violet H and Ada Wilmot took to it like ducks to water, prancing and rattling, sublimely unconscious of how ridiculous they looked. Perhaps this is what Miss M means when she says I am 'different' from other girls — but how can I change my character? It is unfair. You were never sent to boarding-school, so why should I be banished? Do ask your mother to intervene and persuade my parents I should stay at home.

Stormy sunset 18th

To Mabel Gale, Bardsea Hall

...You may be right. Perhaps Miss Harding's classes seem silly because I have grown out of them. As you observe, there are more enjoyable forms of dancing. Floating round a ballroom while clasped in a pair of manly arms must be an improvement on cavorting while banging a tambourine! On the other hand, even when I was Idonia's age I never enjoyed the dancing class with its smell of wet cloaks and hot feet so I am not convinced that growing up has much to do with it.

The news of the week is that Daddy has bought a new horse. This makes three in the stable, so Pixie has moved to new quarters above the cart-shed. He goes up and down the steps very nimbly, but when Mrs Townley came to tea and saw him, her eyes nearly started from her head. The Red Indian (as I call the American nephew) was much amused. Idonia made Pixie go up and downstairs several times to please him.

The new acquisition is a tall rangy mare by Orme. She has a dubious reputation, having whipped round at the start of two steeplechases and refused to take part. Having thus blighted her racing career, she was sold as a hunter. Daddy thinks a few good runs will give her a taste for going forwards rather than backwards. We shall see. Idonia took one look at her and christened her 'Spider', which sums up her appearance quite perfectly.

Whalebone is now in good condition and looks a picture — twice the horse he was last year. I insist on his having twelve

sunset clouds. coming home after a gallop 22nd Oct

getting Whalebone into good condition

spicimens of graceful attitudes i the intervals at the dancing lass Oct

pounds of oats a day, though Jones grumbles and says he'll get above himself, and when they bring me home on a hurdle it won't be *his* fault. How he loves to prophesy doom! It must be his Welsh blood.

As you know, Jones is not the best of whips. He nearly had me and Mother in an awful smash when we went to visit Miss Wilmot. He drove past the house, through inattention, then — in trying to turn the carriage in too short a space between the railings — he succeeded in getting one rear wheel jammed. He didn't realize the obstruction, so almost pulled poor Ladas's head off when trying to swing him round.

Ladas began to sweat and fret and Jones to mutter awful oaths. I jumped out and went to his head and saw at once whose fault it was! It took the three of us to calm Ladas and Jones had to unhitch him before he could get the carriage clear. Mother was quite cross and said he should be more careful...

Saw a heron over the river whilst exercising Whalebone 24th Oct

had a narrow escape from a smash 28th Oct 189

November

To Mabel Gale

...My visit to Aston Bank went ahead despite the weather, but the journey was not without excitement. The floods were tremendous. Near Newby Bridge the line was flooded and the train had to crawl through water up to the pistons. It was a miracle it kept going.

HBT was at Rugby, which was a pity. Tollie kindly let me hunt Barabbas but we had a blank day and never found a fox. There had been a hard frost and the gateways were so badly rutted that my heart was in my mouth in case I lamed him, but he is a clever old horse and managed to keep his feet.

That evening we had better sport with Jacko.

Picture the drawing-room after tea. A tranquil scene: Tollie at her bureau writing letters, Eleanor sewing a frill, me gazing into the fire, Jacko snoozing on the hearthrug. The nurserymaid had just called the children up to bed; the ruins of a sponge cake and some biscuits wait on the tea-trolley for the parlourmaid to fetch.

near Newby Bridge The lines were flooded on the way to Chester 3rd Nov

All is quiet when my ears catch the faintest sound. Scritch-scratch-scritch. Now Jacko hears it too and raises his head, eyes bright, ears pricked. Suddenly he springs up and races in pursuit of a tiny mouse which, deceived by our tranquillity into thinking the room deserted, has ventured out to nibble a fallen biscuit beneath the trolley.

Grrr! Away goes Mousie with Jacko on her brush. After a cracking run from trolley to piano she goes to ground beneath the Chinese chest in the corner, but now our blood is up and nothing will stop us. With Jacko wedged between chest and wall, barking enough to wake the dead, we manage to move the chest. A lamp topples, probably broken, but the pace is too good to enquire.

'Gone Away!' Tollie halloos as she sees Mousie break on the far side of covert.

'Tallyho Back!' responds Eleanor as the quarry doubles on her tracks. She runs the length of the skirting-board and whisks through the door to the hall. Jacko is on the line in a trice, scrabbling over the polished boards with a great cry, but Mousie saves her brush when she disappears down a dark hole in the wainscoting at which Jacko scratches and whines in dire frustration.

A great run, with a point of fifty yards as hounds ran!

To Mabel Gale, 16, Stanhope Crescent, London November 1898

...Weather abominable. Meet cancelled. Horses coughing. Trees bare. Idonia peevish and provoking. Dogs disobedient. Mother away. Lessons just impossible. Miss M brooding.

Why don't you write and tell me life is worth living?

To Mabel Gale

...We woke this morning to a white world. Snow in November — whatever next? Jones predicts the worst winter this century.

It is snow of the deep, soft, wet variety — too heavy to toboggan but pretty as any picture. Jones does not think so and behaves as if the weather has been sent on purpose to try his temper. At once he set to work to spoil the beauty of it by shovelling drifts away from the stable door and laying a straw path which was soon sodden and dingy.

Mr Parker told Daddy that the shepherds at Ayside have been trapping foxes, so we drove over to speak with the culprits and found both the brothers Ferguson at home, with a great pack of tykes outside.

Their tumbledown cottage reminds me of a badger's set and smells very like one, too. Half the window-panes are broken and boarded up; there are unexpected entrances and heaps of rubbish — bones, bottles, broken implements and so on lying about. I stayed outside in the snow while Daddy talked. (He thought the language might be a trifle strong!) Also we didn't want our dogs to provoke a scrap, but I am glad to report that although Punch and Bran looked askance at the home pack and kept their legs stiff and tails very straight as they sniffed noses, they behaved with considerable dignity.

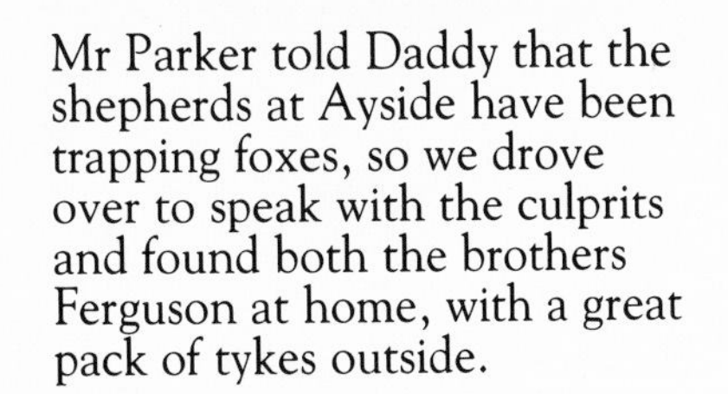

Mother and Idonia have gone to visit Cousin Caroline at Rugeley for a week. I am glad to hear you are coming home for Christmas. Mother has plans to hold a Fancy Dress Dance...

Winter

To Mabel Gale, Bardsea Hall

...At long last a really good day's hunting! You should have come out with us.

The Windermere met at Cark and found a hare so quickly that half the Field was badly left. Major Wilmot and I had a good start and actually saw Puss pulled down by the leading hound after she ran across the railway line and on to the East Plain. One snap and she was dead. The pace was very fast and I listened anxiously in case Whalebone should cough again, but Mr Aysgill's linctus has worked a cure.

The breaker had brought Spider out for the first time since she went to him. He sat her very

a check

the pleasures of galloping over ploughed land, cannonbal of mud clouting you on the head at intervals

quietly with a cigarette in his mouth while she gave a fine display of histrionics at the Meet, alternately rearing and running backwards. Eventually she realised she would not dislodge him, so became calmer.

After killing the first hare we drew the gorse at the far side of the plain. Up jumped another hare and away we went again over some very rough country, with blackthorns and furze-bushes to snatch at one's habit, rabbit-holes to trip the horses and great boulders on a slope so steep that at last even the huntsman dismounted. How I wished I could do the same! Time and again I thought Whalebone was done for, but he found another leg and scrambled along somehow.

As you might expect there was a good deal of grief. Major Wilmot fell into a stream when the bank gave way under his horse, but he wasn't hurt and shouted to me to go on. When at last hounds checked there were only six of us left, all pretty much blown. The huntsman gave me his horse to hold while he cast hounds on the side of a very steep ghyll, but nothing came of it and no one was sorry when he decided to give the hare best.

By this time it was three o'clock and seeing hounds turn towards Grange I thought I had better call it a day. However, before I could put this good resolution into practice, I heard Jem blow away another hare, and couldn't resist rejoining the hunt. I cantered after them along the grass lane that leads to the big dyke, and found Captain Johnson on one of Robinson's hirelings which repeatedly refused to jump the gate at the end of the lane.

He asked for a lead, but no sooner had the horse landed safely than they galloped past us, nearly knocking Whalebone into the dyke. Later, however, he had the grace to come up and apologize for his horse's manners. He says it has a mouth of iron.

Hounds checked at the Maidwell boundary just short of Old Park Farm, and as it was nearly dark I left them...

To Mabel Gale, Bardsea Hall

...Wonderful news! Jerry is home on leave and will come and stay a few days on his way to Scotland. Spider has come back from the breaker a reformed character. I wonder what his secret is? Jones drove her to the station to fetch Humphrey and she didn't shy once. Unbelievable.

More news when we meet on Saturday at Chapel House.

spider in harness Dec 15th

rode into Ulverston put up at The County Hotel met Miss B went to the dancing class which lasted till 2 p.m.. drizzled all the way the way there and poured all the way back

Dec 17th

Xmas day rained hard most of the day —

January 1899

To Mabel Gale

...What a pity you couldn't come to the dance at Chapel House, so missed seeing Jerry. I hope your cold is soon better. You *must* be well for our Fancy Dress Dance. We are all working hard at our costumes and I went to the theatrical costumier in Lancaster to hire a wig — a wonderful powdered creation that makes me look quite ten years older.

Jerry arrived loaded with presents. He gave me a lovely bracelet made of some kind of seeds which the West Indian girls wear. At first I thought him a good deal changed. The moustache gives him an air of gravity which I am glad to say is quite misleading. As soon as he began to mimic his brother officers and demonstrate the native dances I saw he was the same as ever. Even Mother became quite weak with laughter at his antics and didn't mind a bit when he broke a vase while pretending it was full of 'de rum from de sugah-cane!'

After he left the house seemed very quiet, but he gets leave again before Easter and has promised to take me to the theatre in London. This makes the prospect of going South somewhat more appealing.

hounds met at East Plain Cark
stopped from hunting by
the beastly weather 27th

The downpour on Christmas Day meant we ventured out only for church. Afterwards we had our presents. Daddy gave me a handsome new hunting-whip and dear Miss Mackenzie (who left last week after sad farewells) sent me a book of Wordsworth's poems. I shall miss her greatly.

Last night Humphrey and I got up to see the eclipse of the moon, (Idonia wouldn't stir however much we shook her). We climbed the hill to the field just below the Tarn and had a grand view, though we were both shivering with damp and cold. Two meets cancelled this week because of the beastly weather. Yesterday I got as far as the ferry on the way to Windermere where hounds were meeting, found snow and slush had fallen at the head of the Lake, so bunked!

To Mrs Toller, Aston Bank, Cheshire

...I was so pleased with the lovely gloves. Thank you very much. I wore them for the first time to our dance and they were greatly admired.

I must tell you about the dance. We spent all day decorating the hall and supper room with branches and holly and trailing swags of ivy until it looked like an enchanted cave.

The guests began to arrive at eight o'clock, dressed as famous historical personages. Apart from two Napoleons, every one was different. Mother looked beautiful as Cleopatra with golden bracelets and a golden head-dress cut square across the forehead, and a long glittering dress. I went as Madame de Pompadour in a blue silk dress much padded about the hips which we found in the Acting Box. It fitted me pretty well when I had taken in the bodice, and I wore a high white wig from the theatrical costumiers, but found it so unbearably hot that I was glad to discard it at midnight.

Mabel went dressed as Queen Elizabeth I, with farthingale and ruff, and Humphrey as King Arthur. He insisted on carrying an enormous Afghan sword which Uncle William brought back from Kabul although I said Excalibur should be straight, not curved. Daddy preferred his own mess kit. When Mother said he was breaking the rules, he replied that the British Soldier was a historical personage in his own right.

The band from Ulverston played until midnight, when everyone took off their masks and sang 'Auld Lang Syne'. Then we went in to supper, which was quite a feast.

Next week Mother and I are going to London to buy my clothes for school. The list is endless and I am sure I shall never need so many. Then Mother plans to stay with Aunt Carrie for a few days after putting me on the train for Windsor...

February

To Mabel Gale, Bardsea Hall

...Yes, yes, I know. Don't scold me for not writing for so long but I never have a moment to myself in this Seventh Circle of Hell and I have been so miserably homesick that I couldn't summon up the spirit to write — even to you.

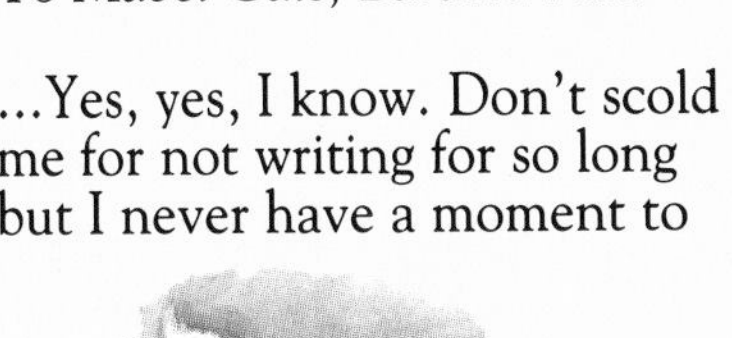

Have you ever been homesick? I used to laugh at Humphrey when he said he couldn't even look at the delicious cakes Mrs Cook sent with him in his tuck-box because they reminded him of home and made him want to howl, so he gave them all away. Now I know just what he meant. The girls here are awful. They chatter and giggle all day long and think I am a freak because I don't care to talk about clothes and marriage *ad infinitum.*

At first I thought it would not be too bad. One or two of the girls were friendly and helped me unpack and showed me where to put my clothes, but all they really wanted was to examine my belongings and make odious comparisons with their own. Everything I have is wrong in some detail, or so they pretend.

Then they asked me a lot of questions about my home, and thought it a great joke when I said I missed Whalebone. They began to call me 'Horsy' and one day when I went into the classroom before lessons I found a horrid picture drawn on the blackboard with 'Horsy in Full Cry' written underneath. I was sure I knew who had drawn it, so I wiped the board clean and when Sarah Westmacott came in smiling, I boxed her ears soundly. Instead of hitting me back she went bawling to Miss Weisse.

For a while I hoped they would send me home in disgrace, but no such luck. Miss Weisse gave me a lecture on the need for self-control. She said it was easy to see I was used to ruling the roost

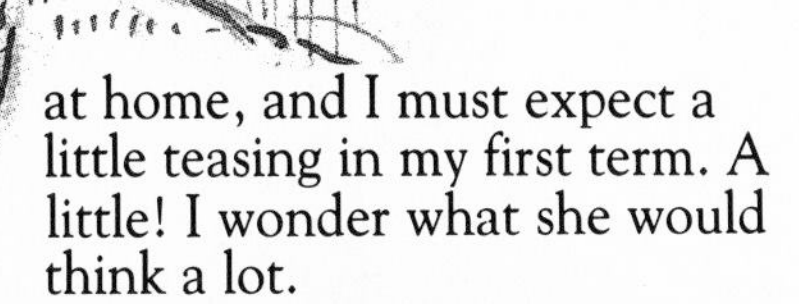

at home, and I must expect a little teasing in my first term. A little! I wonder what she would think a lot.

She called Sarah into her study and made us shake hands, and said if she had any more trouble from either of us she would be extremely vexed.

Now no one talks to me and I am more miserable than ever except in the drawing class and playing hockey. Mr Simmonds the art master says my work shows promise...

To Mrs Sneyd, Finsthwaite House

My darling Mother,

...Thank you for your letter and the pretty handkerchiefs. I am sorry Miss Weisse wrote you a bad report of me. I do try to behave well, but some of the girls do everything they can to provoke me. I will try my best to be friends with them if they will only let me.

Twice a week we go on visits to museums, galleries or places of architectural interest, which I enjoy very much. At Windsor Castle we were just passing the main gate when the Queen happened to drive out, so we waved and cheered most loyally. She was in an open carriage

Went to Windsor saw the Queen

Went to Tate Gallery

drawn by four greys so I saw her quite well, but must confess her appearance disappointed me. She looked like a little black bundle under a large black bonnet. There was another lady beside her and a gentleman in the front. The horses and harness were very fine.

We also visited the Tate Gallery and spent the afternoon copying. Mr Simmonds made some quite complimentary remarks about my sketches and said I should consider taking Art seriously when I leave Northlands.

They have appointed me Captain of Hockey, but it is no great distinction because the other girls play very badly and it is difficult to get a team together — they all make excuses.

Please be sure Jones gives Whalebone plenty to eat in this cold weather. I want him in good condition when I come home. I miss you all very much...

The Captain of the North saves a goal 24th March 1899

Spring

To Mabel Gale, Bardsea Hall,
April 1899

...Oh, how glorious to be home at last! The final week of term was almost unendurable. Every time I saw the great bloated Berkshire daffodils blooming in Windsor I felt an awful yearning for our own pale delicate Lent lilies blowing wild on the hillsides.

Whalebone turned his head and whinnied as soon as he heard my voice in the yard. His delight at seeing me was very touching and I nearly howled. It was kind of you to ride over and see him while I was away, and I am sure the thought that you might descend on him like an avenging

went to get daffodils 2nd April 1899

angel did much to keep Jones on his toes, particularly while Mother and Daddy were in London. Result: he is sleek and round — too fat if anything, but a few good rides will soon remedy that.

Signs of spring are everywhere. I seem to see each tree, flower and bird with new eyes after my long imprisonment. Idonia and I went to get daffodils to send to the hospital and picked two big basketsful in an hour. She has grown — and grown up — a great deal and is now quite a good walker.

Tomorrow Humphrey comes back for Easter...

April

To Mabel Gale, Bardsea Hall

...Was there ever such a beautiful spring? Whalebone and I take long rides in all weathers to make up for lost time. He is now quite fit and galloped a circuit of the racecourse at Cartmel without blowing, but the rain came down so hard I didn't go on for fear of cutting up the ground.

It is strange to think I am already half-way through my holidays. At home the time seems to stretch out endlessly, while at school every day is chopped into short pieces so it is always time to be putting away what you are engaged on and getting out something else. From here Northlands seems remote and unimportant — another world.

I said so to Daddy when we walked to Holker over the mosses, but he wasn't pleased. He told me I must not try to avoid society just because I happen to enjoy solitude, and I should remember that no artist can work in a vacuum. This encouraged me to broach the subject of trying for the Slade School next year, and Daddy said he would have to talk to Mr Simmonds, because there is a world of difference between sketching merely for pleasure and being a serious artist.

Oh dear, how solemn that sounds! I was glad to have the chance to talk alone with Daddy.

He is so calm and thinks things over before giving his opinion. If he approves the idea I am sure Mother will come round to it in time. The question is, am I good enough? Daddy says he can't judge: we must be guided by Mr Simmonds. I feel very excited by this and it has removed a good deal of my dread of going back to school.

Meantime I am adding to my collection of wild flowers, and have passed the two hundred mark. Humphrey and I went to Rusland where we found a thrush's nest and the first violets. We took the dogs with us, but came back without them since they preferred to hunt rabbits in the coppices and were deaf to shouts and whistles.

They returned muddy, guilty, and bedraggled at six o'clock, and were thoroughly scolded and put in the kennel...

To Mabel Gale, Bardsea Hall

...Only a week left — the time is flying. Humphrey, Idonia and I had a lovely walk to Bowness by Graythwaite, and it was so warm when we started we didn't even take coats, although the day before snow had fallen at the head of the lake and the hills glittered in the sun. We found several birds' nests but I wouldn't let Humphrey take any eggs because they were bound to smash in his pocket before we got them home.

While Humphrey was fishing, Idonia and I built a stick-house in the woods in a nice sunny spot and stayed there until five o'clock, when huge black clouds blew up suddenly from the north-west and we had to run for home. Rain pelted down on us and we were all soaked through, with water squelching in and out of our boots. Sarah made Idonia get into a mustard bath at once in case she took a chill.

started at 10 rode to Newlands
Then over the moors to Coniston, down into
the Duddon valley, to Broughton in Furness
round by Foxfield and Ulverston, got back at 5
25th April

Harter Fell

Since there is no grass to speak of yet and it is still too early to turn Whalebone out, Daddy suggested he should earn his keep between the shafts when I go back to school. We put him in the spring-cart in double harness with Ladas; at first I could hardly keep him straight and we progressed in unsteady spurts, with Whalebone edging away as if he thought Ladas undesirable company. The effect was far from comfortable for the passengers. We clung to our seats for dear life as Whalebone sidled and danced; but good old Ladas forged ahead pulling for two and paid no heed to his erratic companion.

We went several miles before Whalebone consented to trot sensibly, but once settled he worked with a will. I felt very proud of my fine spanking pair as we rattled through Newby Bridge. Tomorrow I shall consolidate the lesson by driving them to Greenodd when I go to play hockey for Miss Wilmot's team. Idonia says she wants to come and watch...

H fished we stayed all day in the woods by the river
Humphrey Idonia and I walked to Bowness by Graythwaite came back down the lake 17th
21st Tried Whalebone in double harness for the first time
The Tarn April 19th
played hockey at Grenadd

May

To Mabel Gale, Bardsea Hall

...I have a friend at last. You will laugh when you hear she is the very girl whose teasing drove me to violence with such dire consequences. After that trouble we studiously avoided one another, but this term it so happened that we both missed the 4.45pm train from Paddington and arrived late at Windsor, where the school party had already given us up and left.

Sarah made a fine scene and started to cry, saying we had been abandoned and would have to spend the night on the platform. I left her and went into the town to hire a fly. She was still standing there with her boxes piled up in the pouring rain when I drove back, and looked perfectly astonished when I told her to hop in and look sharp.

Once inside the vehicle she soon cheered up. We could hardly sit stiff and silent for eight whole miles, so began to talk, and then to laugh at our situation. We eventually arrived at Northlands firm friends, to find Miss Weisse greatly agitated by our disappearance, preparing to telegraph our families.

Sarah told the story with embellishments to her particular cronies, with the result that I am now high in favour. She is the strangest creature: tall and willowy with the looks of a Botticelli angel, all soulful eyes and rippling hair, but her temper

is far from angelic. She flies into a tantrum at the least thing, shouts, screams, and throws china...then dissolves into wild laughter. By force of personality she has made herself Queen of Northlands, and woe betide any girl who incurs her displeasure. Yet once she decides to like someone, her affection is nearly overwhelming. I am told her mother is Spanish ; perhaps this accounts for her volatile temper.

Since she took me into favour I have hardly a moment to myself. I am asked — or rather commanded — to sit beside her at meals, walk with her in the park, lend her scarves and gloves, help with her lessons and so on and so forth. Don't laugh, you wretch! You will say it serves me right, but if you knew how miserable was my isolation last term you would agree this train-bearing is a small price to pay for acceptance. You know how jealous mares can be, squealing and kicking when a strange horse is turned out with them? Human behaviour is not so very different.

Sarah is bent on discovering everything she can about me. I answer most of her questions with perfect frankness but am careful not to mention Jerry. Instinct tells me she will peck away at any tender spot until she succeeds in making it bleed.

Today I escaped to walk in the Great Park alone and was rewarded for my stealth with the sight of two fallow does with young fawns, creatures of enchantment. They had bright dappled coats and legs so slender you thought they would shatter at a touch. They stood stock still to stare at me for a long minute, then vanished as if by magic...

To General Sneyd, Finsthwaite House, Windermere

My darling Daddy,

...I am sending you some little sketches I did after the Windsor Horse Show, where we saw the Musical Ride of The Bays among other attractions. They looked so splendid they brought tears to my eyes. I felt very proud to think they were *your* regiment.

There were competitions in tent-pegging and lemon-slicing at which I should dearly have liked to try my skill. The grand finale was the drive by the gun-carriages of the Royal Horse Artillery, whose band played the regimental marches: 'The Duchess of York', 'The Keel Row', and 'Bonnie Dundee'...

Summer

To Mabel Gale, Bardsea Hall
June

...Rehearsals have begun for the end of term play. This is the great event of the summer and Miss Weisse has chosen 'A Midsummer Night's Dream' (which Miss Mackenzie used most daringly to call a 'verra silly play'). Parents and friends are invited to attend and no effort is

spared to make the performance a success. Every girl in the school takes part. The leading roles go to us seniors, while the juniors exercise their Thespian talents as fairies, ladies-in-waiting, attendants and so on. Nearly every afternoon some section of this large cast is summoned to rehearse in the garden if fine or the assembly hall if wet.

You will not be surprised to learn that Sarah has secured the coveted part of Titania, Queen of the Fairies. The head girl, Yvonne Shipley, is Philostrate, Master of the Revels, a role fraught with anxiety on account of her slight stammer. If once she can utter the first few syllables the others follow quite fluently: in her case it is not *le premier pas* but *le premier mot qui coûte*. Miss Elphinstone, who teaches us elocution, has cast me as Bottom. He (you may remember) spends most of one act asleep on stage wearing the ass's head which the mischievous Puck has inflicted on him as a punishment for Titania. (Miss Mackenzie is right: the plot is *verra* silly.)

July Evening

This period of inaction gives me some splendid opportunities for sketching while the other actors plough through their parts. Some of them are slow learners and still don't know their lines after three weeks of rehearsals.

Despite the silliness, the effect is very pretty against a backcloth of flowering shrubs (philadelphus, weigela and diervilla) now in bloom around Miss Weisse's lawn and it is a joy to take off shoes and stockings and feel velvety turf under bare feet...

July

To Mabel Gale, Bardsea Hall

...Mother and Daddy came to watch our play. The dress rehearsal went splendidly but alas, in the performance itself a great many things went wrong.

The weather was very warm but thundery. All afternoon we waited for Miss Weisse to pronounce whether or not we should act in the garden. Soon after luncheon there was a downpour — hope waned, then rose again as the sky cleared.

At four o'clock Miss Weisse took the decision to have the play outside, but during the first scene the drizzle began again.

We carried on bravely, although the audience had to put up umbrellas — and the actors' voices were nearly drowned by the sound of programmes slapping at midges.

First poor Yvonne Shipley muffed her opening lines and stammered so badly she could not be understood. Then Helena was infected with stage fright and had to be prompted from the wings. Hermia covered for her pretty well but there was an

Northlands Tuesday 11th 1899 A Midsummer Night's Dream

awful silence first. Next came a general laugh, quickly hushed, as Puck made his first entrance and it was seen that a wing had come loose and was dragging at his heels so he looked more like a shot pheasant than a sprite.

Worst of all was the moment when I should have been relieved of my ass's head. I only wore it once before, at the dress rehearsal, and found it a tight fit; but this time it caught on my hairpins and no amount of tugging and twisting could drag it off me. The pins drove into my head and nearly made me yell.

It seemed an age while Puck and I engaged in this undignified tug-of-war, and the audience began

Puck and the First Fairy in A Midsummer Night's Dream rehearsing in the garden at Northlands July 1899.

to laugh and cheer. At last Miss Elphinstone hissed at us desperately from the wings, and sent in the dancers who hustled the pair of us offstage.

Behind the philadelphus we managed to pull off the wretched mask, but the atmosphere of the play was ruined...

Langdale Pikes

Next morning betimes we took the train to Crowthorne for Humphrey's Speech Day: my first sight of Wellington College and I thought it very fine. It stands in rolling park-like grounds guarded by an avenue of towering Wellingtonias — The Kilometre, as they call it. The dormitories, or boys' houses, are all named after the Duke of Wellington's generals: Murray, Anglesea, Hope, Beresford, Harding and so on. Jerry was in Orange, I remember, and Humphrey is in Blücher.

After Prayers, Humphrey took great pride in showing us over the many exhibitions: pottery, painting, and photography, mechanics and metalwork — even some jewellery! Two of Humphrey's drawings were on display in the art exhibition, as well as a pottery vase with a

Went to Wellington College Sat 17th
with Mother and Daddy on Speechday
stayed Wellington until Mondey —

To Mabel Gale

...I am in a whirl! My head spins with plans and parties, projects and picnics. I don't know if I'm on my head or my heels. What a glorious thing to be seventeen and in London and in love!

I imagine you smiling to think of your down-to-earth cousin in such a mood. I don't feel down-to-earth any longer. I feel like a giddy butterfly spiralling upwards to meet the sun, careless of whether she burns her wings.

The smile leaves your face. Hmm, this sounds serious. What has got into her? you wonder. This doesn't sound like Barbara! In love?

Read on, fair coz. All shall be revealed.

Where did I leave you? Did I tell you I managed to free myself of that infernal ass's head? (On the way back to our hotel Daddy said it was the first time he had ever laughed aloud at 'A Midsummer Night's Dream'.)

sniping the rearguard

decided list to starboard. We followed him up and down stairways and in and out of arches like a rabbit-warren on a rather grand scale.

H wore boater and tails, which made him look most distinguished; Mother wore her dark-blue grosgrain with the leg o'mutton sleeves, and I had a new green corded silk and a hat that was simply loaded with fruit — Idonia would have called me a walking greengrocer, saucy child that she is!

As if this wasn't enough to protect me from the elements, I carried a very pretty green silk parasol (which unfortunately I left behind in H's study).

Next we attended the display of drill by the Cadet Force and listened to the School Band on South Front. It was a clear blue-and-gold day, not too hot, with a gentle breeze — quite perfect. We talked to — or rather we listened to — Humphrey's tutor and under-tutor, and strained our ears to hear a distinguished old buffer speechifying before presenting the prizes. I caught only about one word in ten: 'God...your country...noble endeavour...wonderful...example ...fine sacrifice...' You know the kind of thing I mean.

I noticed H had become rather silent. He told Mother he wasn't hungry and went to change into his flannels. He also looked a little green but we were tactful enough not to comment. A crowd of people hurried away to Grubbi's, the tuck shop, but we picknicked under the trees at the edge of 'Turf', the main cricket field, sitting on canvas chairs next to Major-General Lygon, who served with Daddy in the Afghan Campaign, and Mrs Lygon. Their son was also for the School, so there was a good deal of chaff.

The Old Wellingtonians won the toss and put the School in to bat. Daddy said he would walk round Turf — I think he was more nervous than Humphrey! I went with him. Every few yards he would stop to talk to friends and introduce, 'My elder daughter, Barbara', until my jaw ached with smiling.

Saw the Eton 8 being coached on the Thames 16th

At last my eye lighted on someone I *did* recognize...none other than Jerry, lounging at his ease with his hat tipped over his eyes as he discussed the finer points of the game. When I tapped him on the shoulder with my parasol he sprang up, quite startled to see me, and asked if he might introduce his friend Lieutenant Harry Carew of the Horse Guards.

That was all. A simple introduction. He smiled. I smiled. We shook hands. He may have said something — I don't remember. But at the moment our fingers touched, a most extraordinary thing happened. I *knew*, without a shadow of doubt, that this was the man I would marry.

Do you think I am mad? Do you believe the sun and wine had gone to my head? Nothing of the kind! Think how often you and I have debated whether there is such a thing as love at first sight. Now I know it exists and I am happier than I have ever been in my life...

The latest things in London July 21st

Now we are staying in London with Aunt Carrie. She took me to the Royal Academy Summer Exhibition where we met Jerry and his friend Lieutenant Carew. Afterwards they took me to tea at Gunters. The ices were delicious and such cakes!

Every morning I ride in Hyde Park like a lady of fashion, but the horses are awfully slow, poor things. We come home at the end of July....

Briar from Miss Weisse's Rose garden

To Idonia, Finsthwaite House

...Humphrey batted very well on his Speech Day and made twenty-six runs before he was given out Leg Before. I didn't see, having turned away, just for a second, to talk to someone. That is the trouble with cricket. It all happens so far away that if you are not watching *all* the time you miss the only exciting moments. Daddy and Mother of course are very pleased and proud of him.

August 3rd
3rd
After riding went up to
the tarn where Mother Daddy
etc were fishing. after tea
partially fell into the tarn
when pushing off boat
found a good deal
of white heath
whilst walking about
on the fell to dry.

August

To Mabel Gale, Bardsea Hall

...How can you doubt me? Of course I am sure. I wouldn't have told even you if we hadn't agreed to share all our secrets. You are not to throw cold water on my dreams. You may as well save your breath if you are thinking of telling me not to count my chickens before they hatch.

He feels the same, I know. Why else would he write to me every day since I left London? To forestall Idonia's teasing I get up early and waylay the postman — I think Mother has guessed why. She suggested to Daddy that he should ask both Jerry and Lieutenant Carew to stay a few days here after they finish shooting grouse in Yorkshire.

Why don't you drive over during their visit so you may draw your own conclusions?

To Mabel Gale

...Harry has gone and his visit seems like a dream. I feel so restless, I don't know what to do. Perhaps if I tell you about his visit I will recapture some of last week's happiness.

I drove Whalebone to Newby Bridge to meet them off the train. It was so late I began to fear they would not come, but at last it pulled in to the platform and they jumped out.

Going home I let Harry take the reins. He handled the horses better than Jerry, being less inclined to play the fool. They told me about their visit to Colonel Ellerby, who gave them a week shooting driven grouse on the moors near Richmond. He also gave a dance for his two daughters, which caused me torments of jealousy until Harry whispered they were neither of them as pretty as me.

Me — pretty! Has Oberon put love-in-idleness on Harry's eyelids? The thought nearly made me crack.

In the afternoon we walked up to the tarn where Mother and Daddy were fishing from the boat. I partially fell in the water when pushing off the boat after tea, and while I walked about to get dry found a quantity of white heath to bring me luck.

Next day was cloudless. All of us except Mother walked over the hill to Grassmere for the Hound Trail and were in time to see them start up Silver How at a great pace. There were tykes from as far afield as Lancaster, but the heaviest betting was on Mr Dunlop's Duster, who finished second. The winner was a hound named Snapdragon, but several farmers lodged an objection, claiming he wasn't Snapdragon at all but a former champion with similar markings, what they call a ringer. There was an awful row.

In the end the winner was disqualified and the prize went to Duster. Jerry was delighted, having backed him at a good price. When we got home he mimicked the whole scene for Mother's entertainment, and she told him he should leave the Army and make his fortune on the stage!

After dinner Harry and I walked down to the lake. The moon made a path of silver across the water, and I won't tell you what he said to me in case you don't believe it.

There was thick mist next morning, but we took a gamble on its clearing and started very early to catch the steamer up the Lake. Idonia and Timmins came with us. After landing at Lowood we walked over the hills to Troutbeck. Harry had never seen sheepdog trials before and was astonished at the dogs' cleverness. The best ones seem able to read their master's mind — as well as the sheeps'.

At noon the mist did clear, giving us another scorching afternoon. We ate our picnic in a lovely spot by the beck. Jerry threw his crusts into the water, and I saw a water-rat creep out very softly and draw a crust into his hole.

Trailhound of A B Dunlop
winner of the Troutbeck hound Trail did 7 miles of hill running in 30 minutes

After the Open class, when the serious drinking began, we started the long walk back to Bowness along the Roman road.

Idonia got a blister on her heel, so Jerry and Harry took turns to carry her.

That night Mother and Harry sang duets at the piano. When he was singing he smiled at me...

17th August
starting up Silver How for the 8 mile course prize £5 won by Robinson's Ruby
18th
sheep dog trials Troutbeck. Hills nearly hidden by rain mists until midday when it cleared
Hound trail Grassmere
some competitors and their Tykes
Daddy Jimmins Idonia and I went by the lake to Lowood landed and walked over the hills to Troutbeck to the sheep dog trials walked back to Bowness by the Roman road
Stagshorn moss

To Mabel Gale, Bardsea Hall

...On Humphrey's birthday Mother invented an excuse to send him to the stables after breakfast with a message for Jones. We were all in the secret and raced to be there ahead of him. When he came, Daddy gave him his present: a horse of his own!

He is a strongly made, clean-legged chestnut six-year-old, just on fifteen hands high, bright bay in colour with a blaze and two white socks behind, called Jack-a-Dandy. Daddy bought him from Atkins's yard in Kendal. He was brought over from Ireland where he is said to have carried the horn in County Waterford where the banks are so narrow that only the cleverest horses can change feet on them. (You know old Atkins's line of blarney!)

Whatever the truth of the matter, he is certainly very well-mannered and as nimble as a cat.

H and I rode over Bigland hill came home by Cartmel 19th August

Took tea up the lake and fished only caught 0 20th

H and I swam in the torn. all had tea there, after Daddy and I fished caught some, only 5 were worth keeping 22nd

He has given Humphrey new enthusiasm for riding, so we have done nearly as much hacking as boating this holidays.

In the low ground by the Lake the flies are terrible, but on Bigland hill where we rode yesterday there was not one fly to be seen and the views were magnificent.

Even better was the sunrise Humphrey and I watched after spending the night on the fell. We left the house at nine-thirty after supper, when it was nearly dark, and climbed up through the black mysterious wood to the Tarn, where we slept rolled in our cloaks like bivouacking cavalry. I woke very often, partly

H and I started at 9.30 to spend the night on the fell near the tarn saw the sunrise at 4 bathed in the tarn and took the boat out then went home to breakfast at 9 23rd August

for fear of missing the dawn, and partly because I kept sliding downhill.

Just after four o'clock the sky began to lighten into a lovely pearly translucence with streaks of primrose and flamingo pink; then the red ball of the sun hoisted over the rim of the hill opposite, with the Finsthwaite Tower in black silhouette, so beautiful I nearly cried.

When it was well up we bathed in the Tarn where the water was warmer than the air. We took the boat out, but the fish must still have been asleep and we caught nothing. At nine o'clock we went home to breakfast...

PS It is no use asking me to describe Harry. You must meet him for yourself. I tried to draw him but it wouldn't come right so I tore up the paper.

September

To Mabel Gale, Bardsea Hall

...Great triumph! Humphrey took Jack-a-Dandy to Ulverston Show and was placed third in the Hunters. He gave a very good show, changing legs perfectly. It was a strong class, but H was pulled in at the top of the line and only gave way to some high-class opposition in the shape of a young horse from Great Ayton, Yorkshire, with a string of wins to his credit, and Mr Micklethwaite's good hunter Nimrod.

Humphrey was delighted beyond speech. As the winners galloped their lap of honour he could hardly hold the rosette in his mouth, so wide was his grin. Now he is determined to have his prize-winning hunter photographed. Will you meet us in Ulverston next Tuesday, when we have an appointment with Mr Goodhew and his little black box? We could ride together afterwards. It seems an age since I saw you...

September 12th Humphrey and I rode to Ulverston had the horses photographed met M Gale all rode over Furness Fells. On the way back saw hens catching flies in a calfs eye and eating them
Helvellyn from the top of Silver How Sept 14th
Whilst out shooting with Daddy found these D got 6 rabbits 13th of September 1899

To Mabel Gale

...Harry wrote today. He says things look bad in South Africa, where Brother Boer is up to his tricks again and making a nuisance of himself. We may have to teach him another lesson in how to behave.

Here at Finsthwaite where the summer continues in its old peaceful way even the thought of war seems remote. I spend a good deal of time sketching flowers for my portfolio, and take long walks with H and Idonia.

Resting at Grizedale Beck on the way to Coniston, Humphrey and I found unexpected treasure in the shape of a fine crop of blackberries under the bridge, already ripe on account of the sheltered spot. These occupied our attention very agreeably for an hour or more, resulting in a somewhat late arrival home with no great appetite for supper.

Next week I go to Aunt Carrie for two nights, and then back to school. Strange to relate, I am looking forward to it...

H and I rested at Grizedale beck on our way to Coniston where we walked to. starting from home at 11 did not arrive there until 5 on account of blackberries

September

DAMARA LAND
BRITISH
Matabele Country
GAZA
SOUTH AFRICA
LAND
S. Sebastian
Sandfontein
Kolahari Desert
Limpopo R
GREAT NAMAQUA LAND
BRITISH Protectorate of Bechuanaland
SOUTH AFRICAN REPUBLIC
Pretoria
Johannesburg
Mafeking
Lorenco Marquez
Delagoa Bay
Swazi Ld
Vaal
ORANGE FREE STATE
ZULU LAND
Orange R
Griquatown
Kimberley
LADYSMITH
Tugela R
Springfontein
Hopetown
Bloemfontein
Basuto Land
Pietermaritzburg
Durban
Bushman Land
Colesberg
Orange River
Storm Bergen
Victoria West
CAPE COLONY
St Helena Bay
East London
Table Bay
Capetown
Port Elizabeth
SOUTH AFRICA

war declared
Oct 1899

Autumn

To Mabel Gale, Bardsea Hall

...The bell for Prayers went early, which generally means Miss Weisse has something extraordinary to announce. When we were assembled she came on to the platform with all the other teachers, looking very solemn, and told us that war has been declared between Great Britain and the Transvaal and Orange Free State.

Generals	Symons	at Glencoe (succeeded by Col Yule)
Colonel	Baden-Powell	.. Mafeking
Col	Kekewich	Kimberley
Sir G	White	Ladysmith
Gen	French	Elandslaagte
Gen	Gatacre	Stormberg
Lord	Methuen	Belmont
Gen	Buller	Estcourt

Everyone felt somewhat shocked; you could have heard a pin drop. Then some of the younger girls began to cry, but most of us felt excited. Prayers went on for longer than usual, and when we were dismissed at last all the seniors crowded into the common room to discuss the news. Nearly everyone has a brother or cousin or friend in the Army. My thoughts were all of Harry.

Instead of our normal lesson in Geography, Miss Dawson made us draw a map of South Africa and mark in the principal towns and geographical features. She said it was important we should become familiar with the country so we would understand the course of the campaign. Julia Stephens got 9/10 for her map, which was nearly perfect.

Not to be outshone, Miss Bellinger abandoned the Wars of the Roses for more recent history and lectured us on the war between Britain and the Transvaal ten years ago. I knew most of it from Daddy, though Miss Bellinger's account of our defeat at Majuba Hill was rather different. I made one attempt to correct her, but when she enquired if I would like to take over the rest of the lesson to air my views, I regret to say I subsided meekly. She can be very sarcastic when she chooses.

At luncheon we had more of the same topic until at last I could stand no more and escaped to walk in the Forest alone. I had the good luck to come upon a rutting stand among the great oaks where a fine fallow buck was parading his antlers before his admiring harem. From time to time he bent his head to thrash the lower branches most savagely, uttering loud hollow groans, and was so absorbed in this pastime that I was able to watch for several minutes before an old doe spotted me and barked a warning...

Oct 1899

The Emperor of Germany's departure from Windsor

Winter 1900

To Mabel Gale, January

...Happy New Year, dear Cousin, and Happy New Century! My own happiness is so great that I want to share it with everyone, but Harry says it is out of the question. After some quibbling he agrees I may share our secret with you: if I didn't I think I would burst.

What secret? you ask. Come, Mabel, can't you guess? After all my hints it should not be too difficult.

No? You give up?

Very well, you shall have it in one simple sentence. Harry has asked me to marry him.

You don't believe me? To be honest, I hardly believe it myself. How long have we known one another? Not more than six months, yet I knew from the start he was the only man I could ever love.

He proposed just ten days ago, under the bare branches of Rotten Row when we rode together while I was staying with Aunt Carrie. I was so surprised I nearly tumbled off my sedate Park hack. Luckily Aunt Carrie was a little way behind and I was able to recover my composure before she came up with us. If she had asked what was the matter, I might have blurted out the truth!

As it was, she gave Harry a very cold look. She doesn't approve of him: I don't know why for he is always most polite.

When we were alone Harry told me we must keep the engagement secret for the present. His commanding officer is a terrible martinet who doesn't approve of his young officers marrying under the age of thirty. Thirty! Harry is only twenty-four. In a cavalry regiment you can't keep a wife on less than a captain's pay and even when he gets promotion Harry will have to ask his colonel's permission to marry. If even a rumour came to his ears before that, Harry might be asked to leave.

I wish he wasn't in such an expensive regiment. The mess bills are very steep and his brother officers play for high stakes, but H says he would not transfer for the world. Now that war is declared there must be a better chance for promotion.

As you may imagine, I came home in a dream. Everything at Finsthwaite is the same, but I am different. I ride and shoot and sketch, but all the time my thoughts are of Harry and I am just filling in the hours until we meet again.

Mother took tickets for the Patriotic Ball which was organized by the ladies of the Working Party. The decorations were very garish: red, white, and blue bunting and flags galore. Miss Harding's pupils displayed their talents in a variety of hornpipes and country dances. How thankful I am all that is behind me!

6th Jan 1900

January

To Mrs Toller, Aston Bank, Cheshire

Thank you so much for the sketchpad and the book on Anatomy which will be a great help to me. You ask if I keep up my sketchbook. Not as regularly as I did in Miss Mackenzie's reign, I must confess. Two days never went by without her reminding me to 'draw my diary' as she called it; but I add something now and then. This holidays there have not been so many parties, on account of the war, so I have done some sketches outdoors despite the awful weather, besides a portrait of Idonia for the Ladies' Club competition.

Last week I went over to Bardsea to see Mabel, and while riding through the Park met this fine cavalcade of brood mares coming down through the trees for their evening feed.

Miss Ada Burton gave Idonia a new ginger kitten to replace poor Tabby who was caught in a trap and killed. She tries to dress him in dolls' clothes, but he is less obliging than Tabby and soon tears them to shreds.

I am so sorry to hear Barabbas died. He was a grand hunter and I shall always remember our

famous six-mile point from Eaton Hall. What a day that was! I have had no hunting this winter. First Whalebone was lame with a prick from the blacksmith, then, as soon as he was sound and had his shoe on, the frost set in so hard that riding was impossible. Jones made a straw ring to lunge the carriage horses, and Whalebone and Jack-a-Dandy were turned out in rugs.

Next week I go to Lancaster to the dentist, and after that back to school...

To Mabel Gale, Bardsea Hall

...Disaster! What am I to do? Mother says I must not see Harry or write to him again. She had a letter from a friend of Aunt Carrie's with awful stories about his gambling debts and how he had treated some girl badly.

I don't believe it. That is, I daresay it may perhaps be true about the gambling, but who cares about money?

Next week he sails with his regiment for the Cape. I must see him before he goes. I don't like to deceive Mother, but I am sure Aunt Carrie's friend's stories are only gossip. At least I should have the chance to ask Harry about them. Jerry says we may meet at his house. (I must confess to a certain curiosity to see inside a real bachelor establishment...something like a fox's earth, I imagine!)

February

To Mabel Gale, Bardsea Hall

...Spare me your reproaches — I know it is over six weeks since I wrote but you can have no idea just how difficult it is to get two minutes' peace in this establishment. The war affects everyone's nerves. Since the recent bad news I have twice walked into a room to find some girl silently weeping. Pray Heaven the tide will soon turn in our favour.

Jerry writes that he has lost his best mare, Meg, who died of the Horse Sickness after the battle at Colenso. She is the third of his stable to succumb. He says our chargers come off the ships so soft from lack of exercise that they are fit for nothing and die like flies. Only the salted ponies belonging to the Boers can stand the climate. (They call them 'salted' if they survive a bout of the fever and it adds greatly to their value).

Saw a Verdant Green.

Now Jerry has only a pony he took from a captured Boer — it is nothing to look at, he says, but hardy — and a remount from the Argentine which he describes as a clumsy beast with no manners.

He has taken part in several engagements and ridden nearly a thousand miles since arriving in Cape Colony. He says the Boer is a dour fighter but lacks discipline — every man is his own general. If he does not care for his orders, he saddles his pony and rides home, but he has one great advantage over us. Having been used since childhood to shoot game from the saddle, he is more than a match for our mounted infantry who can neither ride nor shoot!

Miss Weisse took a party of us to Oxford to see the colleges. We walked holes in our boots and cricks in our necks admiring the architecture of the Bodleian and the Radcliffe Camera, the Martyr's Memorial and more college quadrangles than I can remember. The deer in Magdalen College have magnificent antlers but are stunted and dwarfish in body — I suppose they are inbred: they are certainly not underfed.

Miss Weisse's cousin is a female Don at St Hilda's. She has big round spectacles and high-arched eyebrows which give her an air of perpetual surprise. She was kind enough to entertain some of the girls to tea, but the room was very small so I begged permission to sketch in Christ's Meadow instead, using a new technique that Mr Simmonds showed me.

On our way to the station we saw the Oxfordshire Mounted Infantry on parade. There was cheering and waves from the crowd when they marched past us with the band playing, 'Goodbye, Dolly Gray', but I noticed some of the older women were crying…

Oxfordshire mounted infantry on Parade Feb 25th Oxford.

March

To Mabel Gale, Bardsea Hall

...I have had no word from Harry since he sailed. Has he forgotten me? I cannot eat or sleep for thinking of it. All night long Mother's warnings about his character ring in my head.

I know it was wrong of me to go to his rooms without telling her but I couldn't let him leave without saying goodbye. Every morning I run to meet the postman and then return disappointed. Perhaps he is too busy to write. Perhaps he is dead, or ill, or has found a prettier girl to flirt with him. I imagine a thousand things and cannot attend to my lessons.

Miss Weisse stopped me in the garden and spoke very kindly, asking if I was quite well. I wanted to tell her my worries but couldn't find the words, so said nothing. After looking at me a long time she walked on. Now I wish I had the courage to speak out. Life at Northlands goes on in the usual way — lessons, gossip and bickering interspersed with visits of cultural interest, but nothing seems quite real.

We went to a recital of Schubert songs given by Miss Dawson. When she sang 'The Spinning Song' I knew just how poor Gretchen felt...

Saw the Vandyck collection at Burlington House Feb 1900

Concert at
Northlands
at which
Miss
Fillunger
sung and
Mr Tovey
played Beethoven.
Kreuzer sonata
after Vandyck
from memory
30th March
1900
Maud MacCarthy (aged 16)

To Mrs Sneyd, Finsthwaite House

My darling Mother,

You must not worry, I am quite well only rather tired of being so much indoors, which you know makes me pale. A little rouge would soon mend matters, but what a scandal it would cause!

I look forward to seeing you at the concert at the end of term. There is an exhibition of art and craft, too, and Mr Simmonds has hung two of my paintings in the place of honour. He says he hopes you will let me attend the Slade School of Art when I leave Northlands. He can give me an introduction to his friend Mr Henry Tonks, the Assistant Professor, who is having great success with his pupils. They say he is a wonderful teacher. One of his star pupils is Edna Waugh, who entered the Slade when she was only fourteen. One day Mr Tonks was admiring her drawings and said, 'So you are gong to be the second Burne-Jones?' 'No', she answered very smartly, 'the first Edna Waugh!'

How strange to think this is my last term at Northlands...

Kimberley relieved by Gen French – Feb 16

ought to have been practising when doing this
Felt guilty

Went to a concert at St James Hall. M Halir played

Sir G White VC

6-30
April 16

To Mabel Gale, Bardsea Hall

...Birds are singing, Spring is springing, and Harry has written to me! From living at the bottom of a dark miserable pit where the sun never penetrated, I have now floated up to the rosiest of clouds and feel happy, healthy, and extremely hungry once more. What a difference those two sheets of paper have made to my life!

The family is quite bemused by my altered spirits. Poor Idonia, who has pestered in vain for my help with her 'Circus Act', now finds me directing the whole performance. No longer does Cousin Bee sigh over my lack of appetite and load my plate with tempting morsels. Instead she asks anxiously if I will not get indigestion from over-eating.

The letter arrived just as Idonia and I were setting off for our morning ride. Mother and Daddy had not come back from visiting Cousin Ralph Sneyd, which was fortunate since I

might well have had awkward questions to answer. I ran upstairs to read it alone, refusing to admit Idonia who very quickly tired of whining outside a locked door and went out riding with Jones instead.

It was written in March, soon after the relief of Sir George White's forces at Ladysmith. Harry is no respecter of authority and shines curious sidelights on some of our military heroes. (Naturally I am more interested in personalities than strategy.) He has a low opinion of Kitchener, calling him 'that stinking Egyptian!' but Lord Roberts' energy and resolution have won his approval although Lord R is only 'knee-high to a grasshopper'. General Buller is blamed for a good many military blunders. Harry calls him a fat fool but says that he is a 'sound man in a retreat', which seems a rather two-edged compliment. The Boers object very much to fighting on Sunday, so Harry's commanding officer keeps him busy organizing mule-races and football matches to entertain the men. Once a Boer shell landed in the middle of a football match, but they filled in the crater and carried on playing...

Finsthwaite
April 8 190

April

To Mabel Gale, Bardsea Hall

...It was sad to see Barabbas's stall empty when Idonia and I stayed at Aston Bank. I used to love the way he begged for titbits by twitching his upper lip from side to side, like a man troubled by crumbs in the moustache. He must have been taught the trick when young.

Then, if you gave him a peppermint — he would sell his soul for a peppermint — he used to stick his old Roman nose in the air and wrinkle his lips right back from his teeth to savour the delicious odour. He was a great character. I wish horses' lives were not so short compared to our own. Even my gallant Whalebone is beginning to look his age, though he carries me as well as ever.

Tollie took us to Hengler's Circus in Liverpool and afterwards we were allowed to visit the stables — a great treat. Idonia was in seventh heaven and inspired to new heights of ambition as an animal trainer. Since we got home, Pixie has been compelled to climb on to a tub (which promptly tipped over, giving him and the ringmaster a great fright); jump through a straw hoop (though Jones refused absolutely to let her set it ablaze); and trot in a circle on the lunge-rein with Idonia perched insecurely on his rump. However, he resolutely foils all her efforts to make him lie down and 'Die for his Country'.

Idonia says he is too stupid, but I think him a good deal too intelligent!

Mr Rankin built an enormous bonfire on Cat Craig to celebrate the relief of Mafeking. It was beautiful to see the flames leaping sixty feet at least, while shadowy figures ran here and there heaping faggots on to the blaze.

The Working Ladies had excelled themselves in the provision of cakes and scones. After a good deal of ale had been consumed the singing became rowdy and Mother decided it was time to leave.

No word from Harry for a month. I am tortured by the same old fears. I long to ask Mother's advice but how can I admit I have disobeyed her? What a miserable business it is deceiving those you love and who trust you. I feel torn in two. I have never kept anything hidden from Mother before, but now I am like a cat on a ladder and can't go back...

June

To Mabel Gale, Bardsea Hall

...Daddy and I stayed a week at Aston Bank and Tollie kept her promise to show me some real fishing. In two nights our party caught sixteen sea-trout and ten salmon, two to my own rod! I must say, it makes fishing for perch seem tame.

The river party was made up of Tollie, HBT and his friend Jack Parsons, Miss Llewelyn, Daddy and myself, and we set off at eight in the evening and had a jolly picnic of roast chicken and the first strawberries from the Aston Bank glasshouse while sitting on the bank of the Dee. Then Tollie, Daddy and Miss Llewelyn boarded the boats and we of the younger set went to our appointed places on the Pwll-y-fada and Turn Pools with old William to ghillie for us.

As the light faded a mist crept across the water, but it was by no means dark even at half-past ten. For the first hour the midges tormented me almost beyond bearing. If I pulled down my veil I couldn't see where I was casting; if I tucked it up the little pests settled on my face in swarms. Far from disliking Tollie's oil of citronella they seemed to revel in the smell. I was driven nearly mad with their

biting. It was very still. Not a fish stirred though I changed my fly several times — an awful business in the dusk. William counselled patience.

At last we heard shouts and splashing upstream and knew that Jack, at least, was into a fish. How I envied him! William hurried away to help, leaving me in the grey ghostly gloom which folded round me like a cloak as his footsteps faded away. My old night terror surged back, threatening to overwhelm me, and I nearly flung down the rod and ran after him. Everything was so quiet I could hear bats twittering and feel my pulse beating. When an owl swooped across the pool I thought my heart would stop.

I made myself move along the bank, casting under some bushes in a little backwater just on the edge of the current. A breath of breeze came to drive away the midges, so I lifted the veil off my hot face, and just as I did so felt the smallest, gentlest of bumps against the line, just as if my fly had touched a stone and then floated on.

Heart in mouth, I cast again in the same spot. Again there was a bump, but this time it was more like a tug. There could be no mistake. I imagined the fish cruising round in that still black water, eyeing the strange bedraggled insect and wondering how it would taste.

At my third cast, a number of things happened very quickly. The line swung part way through its arc and stopped. Then with a suddenness that made me jump nearly out of my skin, the fish took. It was a strong, steady pull, quite unlike the wriggling take of a perch. I saw the rod tip bent in so tight a hoop I feared it might snap — but the moment I eased the pressure a little the fish raced away across the pool with the line screaming out almost to the backing. I had to jump from rock to rock in order to keep downstream of him.

You should have heard me shout! I daresay it was no more than a minute or two, but it seemed an age before William came puffing and stumbling along the bank, calling out, 'That's right, Miss Barbara! Well done, Miss Barbara! Keep the rod tip up. Steady now, we'll soon have him on the bank'.

I thought this optimistic and so it proved. For the best part of an hour the fish towed me about the pool, until my wrists ached and my arms were stiff with holding him. Now he would plunge to the depths in a fit of sulks; now break the water with flailing tail, sending silver waves to break on the rocks. Even for a big salmon he seemed uncommonly full of fight. I could not control him at all, and every time William told me to bring him towards the bank he would race away across the pool again. Time and again I thought I had lost him, only to feel the weight on the line the moment I began to reel in.

William was puzzled, but after one of the flailing leaps he saw what the trouble was: the fish was foul-hooked. Instead of playing him by the head, I had him hooked in the back, near the dorsal fin, so he could pull the line about as he pleased.

Nevertheless land him we did afer a titanic struggle that left me quite exhausted. At last he tired and lay a dead weight on the line. I reeled in very cautiously and William waded into the water to net him. As he did so, the hook dropped out: it was a miracle that it had not done so before.

By that time the rest of the party had gathered to watch the contest and they all cheered as we brought him ashore. He weighed thirteen pounds and was the biggest fish of the week.

Back home Dacre and Turner have begun the shearing and the forlorn bleating of separated ewes and lambs fills the summer air...

June 1910

January 1901

To Mabel Gale, Bardsea Hall

...May I accept your invitation to stay a while? I know you have not yet made it, but feel sure you can persuade your mother you are pining for my company! I must get away from home. Peace has abandoned Finsthwaite and my refuge seems to have become a prison. From breakfast till supper arguments rage over my future. Mother wants to present me at Court in full fig of bustle and plumes. Aunt Carrie has promised to give a ball for me at Sherbrooke, after which invitations to all the grand functions of The Season will follow as night follows day. Eligible *partis* will queue for the privilege of dancing with me. I shall be the toast of Ascot, Henley, Lords, Cowes...

'My dear Barbara!' I hear you exclaim. 'How can you possibly object to that? You will have a delightful time. It is every girl's dream.'

Ah, but as you know, I am not every girl and my dreams are very different. I want to stay at home, sketching for all I am worth, studying anatomy (my weak suit) and botany (my strength) until term begins at the Slade — but when I advance this plan Mother's response is invariable. Art School is all very well, but it is not the place to meet suitable young men. How can I tell her I haven't the least desire to encounter any of the species? I can't bear her to be disappointed in me. Time enough when Harry comes home to break the news that we wish to marry. There is sure to be an awful row...

East Plain Cark
A 30 mts run

February

hellebore

To Mabel Gale, Bardsea Hall

...The Queen is dead, long live King Edward VII! We saw the procession pass through Piccadilly on its way to the Abbey. The King was muffled up and looked grim, quite unlike the jovial image displayed in every loyal shop-window.

Since the Court has gone into mourning there will be no presentations until the autumn, and thus at a stroke my problem is resolved. Mother agrees that I may attend drawing classes at the Slade and family harmony is restored!

Daddy has rented a dear little house in Pelham Place where we live very cosily with a cook and two maids. Every morning I trot off to the University with my portfolio under my arm, and enter a wonderful new world where nothing matters but Art...

Feb 2nd 1901
Piccadilly
Funeral procession of her Majesty
Queen Victoria passing through

Mr Henry Tonks

To Mrs Toller, Aston Bank, Cheshire

The Slade is all I dreamed it would be. Sometimes I have to pinch myself to be sure I am awake and working in the very place where such artists as Gwen and Augustus John, William Orpen, Edna Waugh and Ambrose McEvoy took their first steps to fame.

Mr Henry Tonks, the senior drawing master, is the strangest figure, very tall and gaunt with a tremendous bridged nose, blue eyes rather hooded, and deep lines carved between mouth and nose. He looks very much like a bird of prey. Most of the young ladies are in love with him, despite the sharp sarcastic tongue he unleashes on anything that displeases him.

From the moment he dashes into the lecture hall, the place is filled with his enthusiasm. Everyone tries to gain his approval and imitate his style. He was a surgeon before he became an artist, and insists on correct anatomy. 'The direction of the bones!' is his constant cry. 'Observe the direction of the bones!' Though we all know in our hearts that Albert Rutherston is likely to win the Summer Prize for composition, hope springs eternal in the rest of us. I am working on a big canvas of the Kendal Horse Fair — an original choice of subject, at least.

Daddy and I went to Tatts last Sunday in search of a Park hack. We bought the sweetest little chestnut mare with a good deal of Arab about her, very smart and showy. I call her Isabella...

A bit of the
Antique room
of the Slade
with Mr Tonks
teaching
Feb 1901

June

To Mabel Gale, Bardsea Hall

Doddy & I went to the Oxford v Cambridge at Lords

...I can hardly bear to tell you the awful thing I heard at Aunt Carrie's dinner before Ascot.

I was placed between Dr Ross Tod and Herbert Montagu, whom I remembered was captain of cricket the year Humphrey played for the school. Though a year older, he remembered Humphrey well and spoke most warmly of him, asking if he still played and saying he was the best all-rounder of his year.

To make conversation I asked which dormitory he had been in. He said Beresford, which was Harry's house too, so I asked if he knew him.

'Know him?' he said with a rather unpleasant laugh, 'I should say I do! Rather too well for my liking.'

I asked what he meant, and he said, 'Why, don't you know? I thought everyone did by now. The bounder was engaged to be married to my sister, and when he broke it off the poor girl nearly went into a decline. It was lucky for him his regiment sailed when it did, or my brothers and I would have made England a good deal too hot for him.'

Imagine my feelings! For a moment I was afraid I was going to faint, and I must have looked queer because he stared at me in an odd way and said, 'Are you sure you feel quite the thing? Have I said something wrong?'

I covered my confusion as best I could, but the rest of the evening passed in a dream. It can't be true — but if it is, why didn't Harry tell me?

Admiral Drury
Miss Lyon
Mr Sherbro
N
Mrs Ross Tod
Prof Campb
Lady Glamis
Daddy
Lady Lingen
Lady Rivers Wilso
ord Lingen
Lady Sherbrooke
Lord Glamis
Self
Dr Ross Tod
Mrs Sneyd
Sir Rivers Wilson
June
1901

July

Kitty Telfer

28th June 1901

3rd July

To Mabel Gale, Bardsea Hall

...Thank you for sending on Harry's letters. What would I do without you? It makes me miserable to deceive Mother, but I can't bear to tell her now. If she forbade me to write to Harry I think I would die.

He has been seconded to Colonel Benson's force, raiding Boer strongholds at night. He says hunting Boers is capital sport, much better than guarding railways. Once they rode forty miles by moonlight to make an attack on a laager just before dawn, and they bagged every man there.

Next week we hold our Summer Exhibition, after which I shall come back to Finsthwaite. I am longing to see you and have a good talk....

Ida Kynnersleys cat

December

To Mabel Gale, Bardsea Hall

...Another Christmas past, another year about to begin, and still the war drags on. Surely it must finish soon? No one dreamed the Boer would prove such a hard nut to crack. Do you remember how we thought it would be over by Christmas — and that was two years ago?

Harry writes that he had a narrow escape at the battle of Gun Hill, when Colonel Benson was killed. Harry had been sent with a message to Colonel Woolls-Sampson's camp a mile away when the Boers attacked

Benson's rearguard, inflicting terrible losses. He says I must not worry about him because he has a charmed life, but I worry all the same. Now he is under the command of Major-General Bruce Hamilton, who continues the raids on Boer strongholds and burns their farms, which Harry says is a beastly business and not fit work for soldiers.

We would love to come and skate if the freeze goes on. It will be grand to see Jerry. Poor fellow! Daddy was told by Colonel Ellerby that his arm will never be much use again..

This has been a bad winter for hunting. I had a few days before Christmas, but now Whalebone has hardly left his stable for two weeks, and has taken to pawing the door in his frustration...

January 1902

From Idonia's diary

...It has been freezing hard for two weeks but now the thaw has begun. Every morning I put out nuts and suet for the birds and by evening it was gone, every crumb.

Barbara and I drove over to Bardsea to play ice-hockey but we left it too late. The ice cracked most alarmingly, and after we had played a little we had to stop.

Jerry was there but he didn't skate because his arm is in a sling where he was shot. His face is brown and he is thin. He didn't laugh as he used to, even when I teased him. Barbara sat with him and talked for a long time. On the way home she was crying, but when we got near the house she dried her eyes and made me promise not to tell. I asked what was wrong but she wouldn't say, only that Jerry had given her very bad news.

Tomorrow she is going hunting although Jones is cross. He thinks the ground too hard. Barbara called him a silly old man and made him give Whalebone a lot more oats...

Susan 26th Jan

Skating at Bardsea January

Went to the Highshut Tuesday 28th

April

To Mabel Gale, Bardsea Hall

...The nurse is sitting by my bed. She says I have been ill. Idonia brought me a big bunch of daffodils. I asked if Whalebone had gone out to grass yet but she began to cry and the nurse sent her away.

Her name is Nurse Ellen Sharpe. I asked if she cut herself and she looked cross. She said making insolent remarks will not help me get well.

She asks who I am writing to but I won't tell her. She asks a lot of questions but I don't answer. I am too busy to talk to her. Soon the war will be over and Harry will come home. I must be quite well before he comes...

Millendrath from Bray Cornwall

The Epilogue

Barbara never recovered her health, nor did Harry ever return. Little is known about the nervous breakdown which cut short Barbara's active life soon after she finished her sketchbooks. Her mother spoke vaguely of a fall from a horse, and so effectively discouraged discussion about her elder daughter that the next generation grew up unaware of the nature or cause of the illness.

In her early twenties Barbara was confined to a nursing home where she died half a century later. A riding accident? A disappointment in love? Whatever the cause of her tragedy, all that remains of a life which began with such bright promise are these glimpses of a Lakeland childhood.

The End

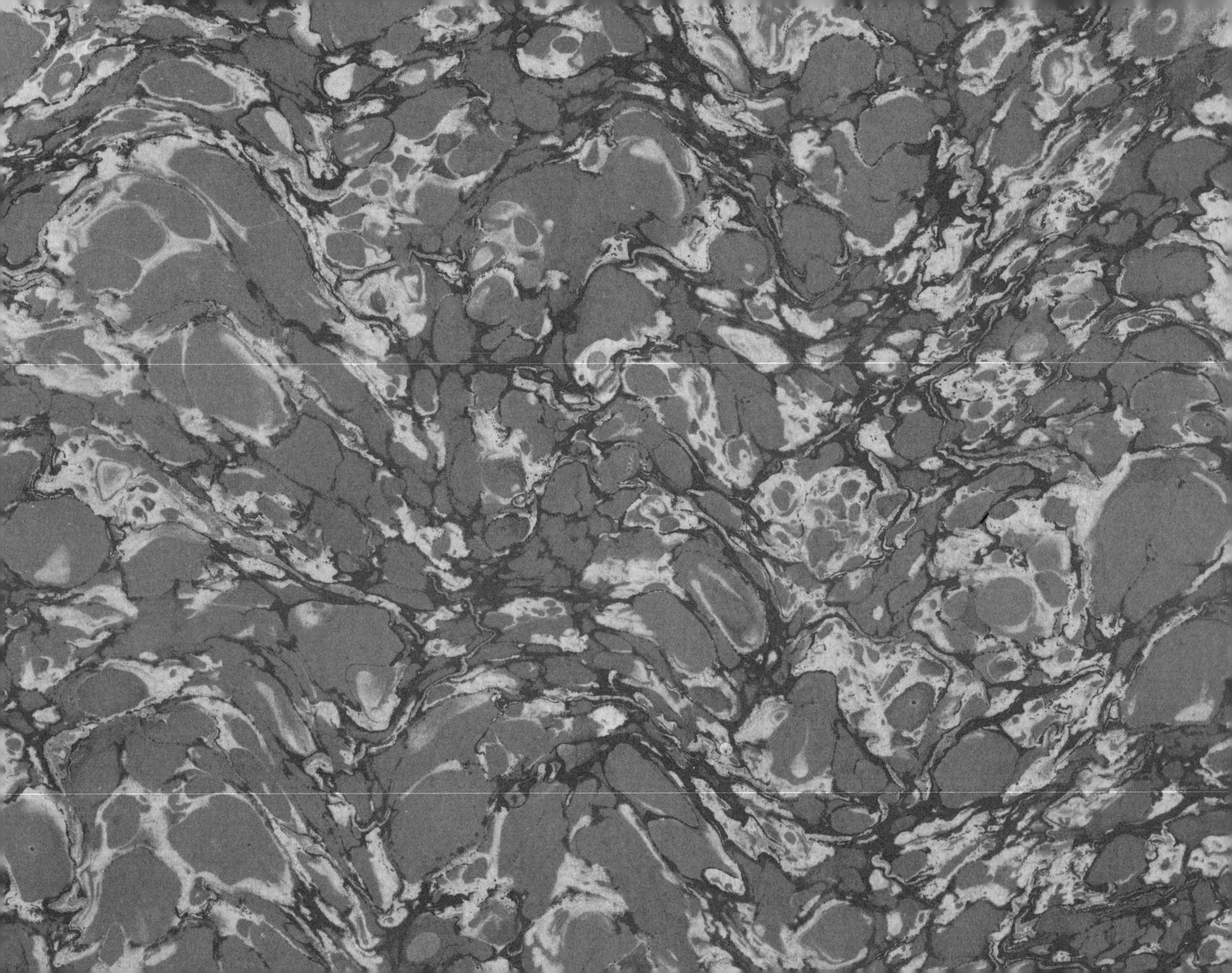